END OF THE LINE

Frank and Joe climbed onto the roof of the speeding train in pursuit of the man who had so far eluded them. The man was far ahead, running toward the end of the train.

Joe reached the accordion gap between the baggage car and caboose and hurled himself over. Now he was only a few yards behind the man.

Then it was Frank's turn to jump. He hit the caboose roof, staggered, then steadied himself. Ahead of him, their quarry was standing upright at the far edge of the caboose roof, staring down at the tracks below.

As Joe approached him, the man suddenly swung an arm back and caught Joe in the chest.

The unexpected blow knocked Joe off balance. He tottered back, his arms windmilling wildly as he fought for his balance on the slippery roof.

"Joe!" Frank yelled, running for his brother. But Joe fell, tumbling toward the side of the roof—and then he went over!

Books in THE HARDY BOYS CASEFILES® Series

Available from ARCHWAY Paperbacks

THE HARDY BOYS CASEFILES NO. 57

TERROR ON TRACK

FRANKLIN W. DIXON

AN ARCHWAY PAPERBACK
Published by POCKET BOOKS
New York   London   Toronto   Sydney   Tokyo   Singapore

AN ARCHWAY PAPERBACK *Original*

An Archway Paperback published by
POCKET BOOKS, a division of Simon & Schuster Inc.
1230 Avenue of the Americas, New York, NY 10020

Copyright © 1991 by Simon & Schuster Inc.
Produced by Mega-Books of New York, Inc.

ISBN: 0-671-73093-2

First Archway Paperback printing November 1991

10 9 8 7 6 5 4 3 2 1

THE HARDY BOYS, AN ARCHWAY PAPERBACK
and colophon are registered trademarks of Simon & Schuster Inc.

THE HARDY BOYS CASEFILES is a trademark
of Simon & Schuster Inc.

Cover art by Brian Kotzky

Printed in the U.S.A.

IL 6+

TERROR ON TRACK

Chapter

1

"I THINK we've grown ourselves a tail." Frank Hardy's lean face tightened as he gazed into the rearview mirror. Just twenty minutes earlier he'd pulled out of San Francisco International Airport. A long black sedan had been following the car ever since.

"The ever-popular big black car." Joe, Frank's younger brother, turned his blond head and grinned as he looked out the rear window. "Whoever the bad guys are, they're pretty traditional."

"Make that pretty conspicuous." Frank returned his gaze to the road ahead. California's winding Pacific Coast Highway required a driver's complete attention.

Right then the sedan sped up and shot past

their car, racing southward. Tinted windows prevented the Hardys from seeing inside.

"The license plate is covered with dust—I couldn't read it," a deep voice sounded from behind the brothers.

Frank glanced into the rearview mirror at the speaker. Leave it to his dad. He still took license plate numbers—an old New York City cop habit, Frank thought. That was what had made his dad a good cop—and nowadays, a good private eye. Fenton Hardy handled lots of cases and sometimes brought his sons in on them.

"Okay, Dad, we've put up with this secrecy business for too long. How about telling us what this trip is really about?"

"Yeah, Dad, what's the mystery?" Joe asked. "I don't know if you should trust Frank at the wheel if he doesn't know where he's going."

Frank ran a hand through his brown hair and gave his younger brother a sour look.

"Okay, okay, I'll tell," Fenton Hardy said. "Has either of you ever heard of Professor Arthur Driscoll?"

"Nope," Joe said.

"*I* have," Frank answered. "He was all over the covers of the science magazines recently. People were saying that he's done for chemistry what Einstein did for physics."

Fenton nodded. "Well, he's our client."

Joe whistled. "This is beginning to sound like a big one."

Frank had suspected that already, since Fenton was being so secretive about the case. Professor Driscoll must be in major trouble.

"So what exactly are we supposed to do?" Joe asked. "Are we bodyguards?" Muscles bunched under his T-shirt.

Frank grinned. As usual, his kid brother was eager to get into the middle of things.

"We're going to protect the professor and a virus he accidentally developed," Fenton Hardy said.

"Accidentally?" Joe repeated, puzzled.

"We'll get the whole story when we reach the Starland Research Facility—it's about ten miles up the road here," Fenton said.

"Too bad the road isn't a straightaway," Frank commented. He had to work to keep the car in its lane as the road twisted and curved like a gigantic snake. To make matters worse, the traffic was getting heavy. Frank had to leave it to his dad and brother to enjoy the scenery. To the left were tree-covered hills, while just beyond a guardrail to the right was a dramatic drop-off to the Pacific Ocean, hundreds of feet below.

When Frank rounded the next curve he saw a straight stretch ahead with a rest area off to the left. He also noticed a big black sedan in the rest area. Was it the same one that had

3

followed them? That big boat looks out of place, parked among the station wagons, picnic tables, and playing kids, Frank thought.

"We were called in because there was an attempt to steal an important vaccine," Fenton went on. "We're supposed to make sure that whoever is after the vaccine doesn't get it."

"Why swipe vaccines?" Joe asked.

"They can represent millions of dollars worth of time and effort—and a hefty research shortcut to an unscrupulous company if it got its hands on one."

"I guess we'll have to make sure that doesn't happen," Joe told his father.

Frank was hardly listening. His mirror showed that the black sedan had rejoined the flow of traffic, just two cars behind their rental model. "We've got the same company again," he said.

Fenton craned his neck out the back window as Frank took them into a sharp curve.

"He's picked a weird spot to try to pass us," Joe said as the black car tried to overtake them through honking traffic. "Wait a second! That's a gun!"

Joe had seen the business end of enough pistols in his adventures with Frank. He immediately recognized the snout of a gun.

So did Frank. He sent their car angling

4

away from the attacking vehicle and onto the gravel shoulder on the right side of the road.

Frank slammed on the brakes, and the rental car went into a sharp skid. Frank fought to regain control, steering into the skid before they took off over the cliff edge. The guys in the black sedan didn't even need to shoot to kill them—the fall would take care of that!

Plumes of gravel whirled up from under the tires as the guardrail loomed closer. Just as Frank was convinced they were going over, the rental car jerked to a stop, just tapping the rail.

For a couple of long moments, the Hardys sat in silence, listening to their heartbeats return to normal. Finally Joe said, "Do you get the feeling that maybe those guys don't want us to go to Driscoll's lab?"

"Well, at least they didn't hang around to see what happened to us." Frank turned the key to restart the rental car's engine. "Who knew we were coming out here?" he asked his father.

"Professor Driscoll called me in strictest confidence," Fenton Hardy replied. "He believes secrecy is the only defense. I didn't tell anyone about our travel plans—not even him."

"So we're up against someone who probably has a tap on the professor's phone and enough of an organization to find out how we were getting out here.''

"I didn't see any great need to cover our tracks," Fenton acknowledged with a lop-sided grin. "So I guess it was easy enough for anybody to pick us up at the airport. Let's just get to the professor before anything else happens.''

Frank smiled to himself as he drove on. This wasn't the excitement he'd planned for that day. Before his father had recruited him, Frank had been expecting to spend the evening at a concert with his girlfriend, Callie Shaw. Now Callie was using his ticket to take a mutual friend, Chet Morton, with her. Knowing what a snack-aholic Chet was, Callie would be lucky to catch any music above Chet's munching.

"Take a left at the next junction." Fenton's words cut into Frank's thoughts. Frank saw the intersection coming up ahead. He slowed down, putting on the turn signal.

They swung off the highway and onto a road that led to a huge compound surrounded by a high, chain-link fence. Beyond the gate Frank could see several large buildings, but to get to them, they'd have to pass the two guards blocking the drive.

Fenton rolled down his window as Frank brought the car to a halt. One burly guard continued to stand in their path. Frank noticed that the man wore a sidearm and that his hand hovered over the holster. The other guard, also armed, approached the car with a clipboard.

"I'm Fenton Hardy," Fenton said, introducing himself. "I believe Professor Driscoll arranged clearance for my sons and me."

"That's right, sir," the guard said, checking a list on his board. "The professor is in Building Four-A." He pointed to a large white structure about sixty yards away. "I'll still need to see some ID before I can admit you."

Fenton produced his wallet.

"Your sons, too, sir."

As soon as the guard was satisfied, the gate was opened and Frank drove through.

"They're really into security," Joe commented.

Frank pulled up to the building the guard had pointed out and into a parking space. Several people passed, all laughing and talking. Frank noticed they all were wearing white lab smocks.

Fenton slid out of the car and headed for the entrance, the boys at his heels.

A quick talk with the receptionist and they knew that Professor Driscoll was in Lab Twelve at the end of the hall.

Frank's brown eyes took in laboratory after laboratory as they headed down the corridor. Tables were covered with test tubes, beakers,

Bunsen burners, and other more high-tech equipment.

He had almost caught up with his father at the end of the hallway. The door marked Lab Twelve swung open just then to reveal three men in white lab coats. In the lead Frank saw a man with a long, hawkish face. Sandwiched between him and a shorter, stocky man was a thin, elderly man with tousled gray hair and wire-rimmed glasses.

"Professor Driscoll!" Fenton called out.

Frank watched as the elderly man looked up, and was shocked to see blood on Driscoll's lower lip.

The tall leader and the stocky man seemed to be equally shocked—but for different reasons.

"It's Hardy!" the tall man said, plowing into Fenton with enough force to send him stumbling back into his boys.

The two men whirled and bolted for an exit door opposite the lab entrance.

Caught off guard, Frank staggered back under his father's weight, barely able to support him.

Professor Driscoll leaned against the wall, trembling. "Th-they were trying to steal the vaccine," he gasped.

Fenton Hardy was already out the door in hot pursuit. Joe had moved almost as fast, and only Frank trailed behind. The sunlight outside seemed brighter than the lab fluorescents, making Frank blink. He did see Joe chasing the stocky man, who had cut to the left. Fenton was being badly outrun by the tall guy, who was heading for the right-hand corner of the building.

Splitting up to double their chances of escape, Frank thought. Well, I'll help Dad with the tall one. He quickly passed Fenton and settled in for a long-distance chase. The tall man could run, and it took all of Frank's speed to keep him in sight.

The man took the corner, and seconds later Frank did the same. His shoes smacked the sidewalk, his arms pumped. Now the man was heading for the front of the building. Frank glanced toward the gate, trying to see if the guards had noticed but realizing a row of trees and a hedge blocked his view.

Frank had cut his quarry's lead considerably by the time the man rounded the end of the building. The hawk-faced figure ran into the parking area, then halted, spinning back toward Frank. Frank leapt, trying for a diving tackle.

Panther quick, the tall man dodged, and Frank came down hard on his elbows and knees. Before he could get up, the man had kicked him in the ribs. Frank's breath whooshed out in a gasp of pain. He rolled away, trying to avoid his quarry's feet.

The tall man didn't continue the attack,

though. He just stepped away. Frank didn't bother to wonder why. It took all his will to ignore the pain screaming in his side as he pushed himself up on one elbow.

Then he heard the growl of an engine and knew why his opponent had left. Frank glanced over his shoulder to see an all-too-familiar black car come roaring up. The last time he'd seen it, he'd been playing bumper cars with it in his rental sedan.

Now it was just him and several tons of steel on a collision course.

Chapter

2

FRANK THREW HIMSELF to the right, and the tires missed him by inches. Rubber squealed as the car braked. Frank wobbled to his knees.

The tall guy he had been chasing flung open the back door, jumped inside, and the black car peeled away.

Rising painfully and holding his side, Frank could only glare in frustration as the car escaped. Fenton Hardy rounded the corner just then as Joe jogged up from the other side, rubbing his jaw. "That guy sucker-punched me," he announced. "Did he get away?"

"Yeah, he must have been driving that black sedan." Frank nodded toward the gate, where the car was just cruising through. He was tempted to try to shout for the guards to stop the men, but they were too far away.

"You boys okay?" Fenton asked.

"It only hurts when I laugh," Joe said. "And I don't think I'll be doing that for a while."

"I'm positive that that was the car that tried to run us off the road earlier," Frank said. "Did you see anyone else in it?"

"I was too busy seeing stars," Joe admitted.

"Let's check on the professor," Fenton said, heading back to the building.

Frank stared out the main gate. If only they'd gotten a license number! He had caught the first three digits this time, and filed them away. He took a step toward the lab, then realized that a huddled crowd of workers was staring nervously at him and Joe.

"Scientists!" Joe muttered. "They stood there like sheep while you almost got killed."

"They use their heads, not their muscles," Frank said. "We didn't look like geniuses out there, you know."

The white-smocked personnel cleared a path as the Hardys headed for the door. Just as Joe was about to grab the handle, an alarm blared, making him jump. He and Frank stepped inside then to find his father and Professor Driscoll standing beside the receptionist's desk. She was on the phone to gate security, talking loudly to be heard over the sirens.

"Did you see which way they headed? At least you can tell the police that." She hung up. "Professor, I don't know what to tell you. Security says the men had full government IDs. And their names corresponded with those on the visitors' list. Security is calling the police now, though."

"Thank you." Driscoll gingerly touched his lower lip. The bleeding had stopped, but it was already swollen.

"These are my sons, Frank and Joe," Fenton introduced the boys to the scientist. "Is there somewhere we can talk until the police arrive?"

Driscoll nodded. "My office. Gwen," he said to the receptionist, "you know where to find us." He led the way down another hall to an office crowded with books. Driscoll sat behind the small desk. Fenton took one visitor's chair, Frank the other. Joe stood and leaned against the wall.

"I can't believe this actually happened." Driscoll shook his head. "Imagine trying to steal a medicine in broad daylight."

"Tell us what happened, from the beginning," Fenton said. "You gave me the short version on the phone yesterday, but I think we need to hear it all."

The professor spread his hands on the desk and silently stared down at them as he collected his thoughts. "It began the night before last. Someone broke into my lab and tore it apart. I suspect they were looking for my serum."

"What serum?" Frank asked.

"It's the result of my latest research," Professor Driscoll stated. "I'm sure you've heard of the new virus that appeared in Asia about two years ago. Fatality is so high, the Indonesians just call the virus *Mati*—Death."

Joe glanced up. "I've heard about it," he said. "Some people are calling it a biological weapon on the loose."

Driscoll shook his head impatiently. "The hard facts are that our government is worried about an outbreak of the disease occurring in this country. Nine months ago they asked me to work on a vaccine and fully funded my research."

"And you've developed one?" Frank was impressed. Driscoll's work could save countless lives.

The professor nodded. "I have—and word has gotten out already. There are many people who'd like to get their hands on my serum. You understand that any company that markets the vaccine will make hundreds of millions of dollars."

Joe whistled. "And where there's that kind of money to be made, there are people who will do anything to steal the vaccine."

"And others who'll pay almost anything for

what they stole, no questions asked," Frank added.

Driscoll nodded. "You do understand."

"So we have to make sure the bad guys don't get their hands on your serum." Joe shrugged. "Doesn't sound too hard."

"That's not all." Driscoll sighed again. "There's a complication."

Frank remembered something his father had said on the way to the lab. "Right. Dad mentioned that you'd accidentally developed a virus."

"Developed isn't the right word," Driscoll objected. "While I was experimenting with *Mati,* the virus mutated. It happens sometimes during research."

Joe grinned. "I've heard of mutant superheroes, so why not a mutant virus?"

"You've probably had one," Frank said. "Every new strain of the flu is a mutated virus. That's why they're all so hard to combat."

"But this mutation is far more deadly than any known flu," Driscoll said. "And it's considerably more deadly than the original virus."

Joe's grin disappeared. "This doesn't sound like good news."

Fenton leaned forward in his chair. "Have you developed a cure for this mutated virus?"

Professor Driscoll shook his head. "I need help. There's an expert in Chicago who has agreed to lend a hand. All I have to do is get the virus to a facility there." He paused. "That's where you come in."

Joe glanced at his father. *"We're* supposed to deliver a killer virus? Why don't we call in the army and let them take it there in a tank?" He was only half joking.

"I don't want more strangers involved," Driscoll said firmly. "Remember, those men who got in here today supposedly had government IDs. I wanted someone I could trust— and luckily, I'd met your father some years ago." He glanced at Fenton. "This situation is very difficult. Both my ~~mutated virus~~ strain and my serum have to go to Chicago."

"Both the serum and the virus have to go?" Frank said.

"My fellow researcher has to see what I've done already," Driscoll explained. "We hope to use my serum as the basis of an improved vaccine that will work on the new virus as well."

Fenton nodded. "Can you tell us anything at all about the people who are after your serum?"

The professor shrugged. "Only that they seem to be very well organized, and they know a lot about my work. They knew which lab to search, but luckily the vials were stored in an office safe that night."

"What about the two men who tried today?" Fenton probed. "What did they say?"

"Not much. They showed up only a few moments before you did. The tall one demanded my specimen vials. When I refused to turn them over, he hit me." The professor's hand again went to his lip.

"What happened then?" Frank wanted to know.

Driscoll looked down. "I lied," he said. "I told him the vials were in another room and I'd take him there. That was when we bumped into you."

Joe stared at the scientist with new respect. "You took quite a chance."

"Not really," Driscoll said. "Security has been doubled since the break-in. I figured I'd be able to alert the receptionist and have guards all over in an instant."

"Which could explain why the two men didn't use guns," Fenton said. "They figured on outwitting security, not outfighting it."

"Whoever they are, they do sound like pros." Frank leaned back in his chair, almost touching the door of the cramped office. Suddenly, he became aware that the doorknob was turning.

He was on his feet in an instant, jerking the door open.

Two men in white lab coats were framed in the door. The one who'd had his hand on the knob was in his twenties, thin, with long black hair. He totally ignored Frank, his intense blue eyes focusing on Professor Driscoll.

"Dad!"

The professor smiled. "It's all right," he told Frank. "This is my son, Andrew, and my assistant, Curt Loring."

Frank stepped to one side, studying the assistant. Loring was a stocky man with curly brown hair. He stared curiously at the Hardys as he came in.

"We were in radiology when we heard the news." Andrew crossed anxiously to his father. "Are you all right?" Driscoll nodded.

"If the research was as fast as the rumor mill here, we'd be world famous." Loring showed square white teeth when he grinned.

"Let me introduce the Hardys—Fenton, Joe, and Frank," Driscoll said.

"Oh. These are the ones you told us about," Andrew said with a smile. "Boy, am I glad to see you. We really need your help."

"I've told you before, Professor, we should be handling this ourselves, without bringing in outsiders." Loring glanced at the Hardys. "No offense, but I don't know you guys."

"We've been through this before, Curt." The professor looked tired.

"We're supposed to be a research *team*," Loring responded. "But you made this decision without consulting me."

18

"Why should my father check with you?" Andrew wanted to know. "It's his vaccine."

"We all made contributions to the discovery," Loring said stiffly.

"Curt, I'm sorry if you're offended," Professor Driscoll said. "But the Hardys will oversee getting the serum to Chicago."

"Just as long as I get to go, too." Loring's fleshy face was set in hard lines. "I have a stake in this."

"I think we should leave the job to the professionals." Driscoll touched his swollen lip. "It could get very dangerous."

Curt Loring didn't respond. He just wheeled around and stalked out of the office.

Driscoll sighed. "I must apologize for Curt. He's a fine chemist and a hard worker, but he can be very testy."

Fenton Hardy rose and closed the door. "Now we have to plan how we'll get the vials to Chicago." He looked at Driscoll. "I assume you want to leave as soon as possible?"

"Definitely," the professor replied.

"Maybe we should try the old shell game," Frank suggested.

"The what?" Driscoll asked.

"It's a game where you hide a pea under one of three shells, shuffle them around, and have someone try to guess which one has the pea."

"An old trick but effective," Fenton said.

19

"It's exactly what I suggest we do with the vials. By separating, we can throw the thieves off the track of the real courier."

"How?" Andrew asked.

"Your father and I will take the next plane to Chicago. You and my sons will board the next train. Anyone tailing us will have no idea who actually has the vials."

"Who will be carrying the materials?" Professor Driscoll wanted to know.

"None of us." Fenton grinned. "We're hiring a private security firm to transport the vials by truck."

"Ah. Clever." Driscoll rubbed his hands together. "But I'm not sure I like the idea of being separated from the vials."

"Do you have a better suggestion?" Fenton asked.

Driscoll could only shake his head.

"I'm glad, because I'm calling the airline right now," Fenton responded with a smile. As soon as he finished his calls, he handed a piece of paper to Frank. "Here's a list of train departures. Right after we've talked to the police, you, Joe, and Andrew head for the train station."

Frank grinned. He was learning to think like his dad.

The phone on Driscoll's desk rang. "Yes? Oh, send them in." The professor raised his eyes. "That was the receptionist. The police have arrived."

Frank found himself talking to a young detective as his father and Joe spoke to other officers. The first thing Frank mentioned was the partial license number he'd gotten. In less than half an hour—while he was still going over history—the police found the black car.

"It was abandoned about two miles from the lab," the detective said. "Of course, it was stolen."

When Frank finished giving his statement, he found his father and Joe waiting. "Joe has already shifted his suitcase and yours into Andrew's van," Fenton said. "You can leave as soon as Andrew joins you. He's saying goodbye to his father."

A moment later Andrew came out the doors, carrying a slim black briefcase. "A little camouflage," he said with a wink, leading the way to a brown late-model van.

"I'll be in touch," Fenton said as the boys climbed into the van. "You can leave messages for me at the Lakeshore Grand Hotel in Chicago."

Frank waved out the window as they pulled away, out the gate, and back on the Pacific Coast Highway. "Mind if I stop off to pack a bag?" Andrew asked. "My house isn't far from here."

He drove four miles, then turned off on a

side road leading into dense woods. The trees turned the road into a green tunnel, with an opening hundreds of yards ahead.

"Got something to drink at your house?" Joe asked. "All of a sudden, I'm thirsty as a—"

He never got to finish the sentence. The sharp *crack!* of a rifle sounded twice.

Then the van's windshield became a maze of hundreds of cracks with two large holes.

Chapter

3

"WATCH OUT!" Andrew cried, swerving the van to reverse direction.

A third bullet took out the driver's side window, and Andrew—unhurt but terrified—cut the wheel too hard. For a horrible second the van teetered in midair, the left wheels feet off the ground. The van was on the verge of tipping over.

Andrew's face was stark white as Frank watched him wrestle with the wheel. Finally he did manage to get the van righted with a bone-jarring crash. Frank bounced around in his seat before he felt them sliding toward the side of the road and a deep ditch. There was barely time to brace himself before they went in. With a muffled crunch, the wheel under

Frank's seat broke off. They lay canted at a weird angle.

Andrew started to open his door, but Frank held him back. "You want to give that sniper a new target?" he snapped.

"We can't stay here!" Andrew's eyes were wild. "What if a bullet hits the gas tank?"

From the rear of the van, Joe called, "I've got the back door open. We can get out this way."

They hoped the body of the van would screen them from the shooter as they scrambled out from the tilted exit.

"We can't stay here forever," Joe said from his half-crouch at the rear of the van. "The sniper could be moving to a new position."

"Hold it," Frank said, cocking his head. "I hear the sound of a car engine. It's coming this way."

They peered around the edge of the van to see a red station wagon heading toward them, an elderly woman at the wheel.

"That's Mrs. Lubben, our neighbor," Andrew said. "She was a good friend of my mom's before she passed away. She'll give us a lift."

He stepped onto the road, flagging the car down.

"Are you nuts?" Joe hissed. "You could get yourself killed."

There was no shot, though. The woods were silent.

Mrs. Lubben pulled over, staring at the van. "Andrew? Are you all right?"

"I'm fine, Mrs. Lubben. So are my friends." He gestured to the van. "We blew a tire, and I lost control."

Frank joined Andrew, scanning the trees across the road. Not so much as a bird fluttered. Great, he thought. The sniper realized he'd blown it and split.

Andrew paid no attention to the trees. He was speaking with Mrs. Lubben. "We were about to leave for Oakland to catch a train," he said. "I know it's a lot to ask, but could you give us a lift to the station?"

Mrs. Lubben thought for a moment. "Yes, I can. My husband won't be back until late, and I have no pressing appointments."

"Thanks!" Andrew said gratefully. He joined the boys to get their luggage.

"What about the bag you were going to pack?" Joe asked.

"I'm not hanging around now," Andrew responded, grabbing his briefcase.

Mrs. Lubben had already released the trunk lock. "Put the bags back there," she said.

Joe smiled as he transferred their luggage into Mrs. Lubben's car. The woman may have saved their lives by coming along just then and scaring the sniper off.

As they headed north on the Pacific Coast

Highway, Joe glanced out the back window. No sign of a tail.

"It's two o'clock now," Frank said as he, Joe, and Andrew left the ticket counter and headed for the platform. "Dad's been in the air for half an hour. Too bad we can't call him about our little adventure." He glanced at the schedule in his hand. "Our train doesn't leave until three. That leaves us lots of time to kill."

"Do you have to put it that way?" Andrew asked. "Anyway, I know how to use the time. I'll shop for what I need for the trip."

"We'll go with you," Joe said.

"I can shop for shaving cream by myself," Andrew responded. "Who's going to try something in downtown Oakland?"

"I'd hate for you to find out the hard way," Frank said. "Let us keep an eye on you."

"I'm a big boy." Andrew's voice turned sarcastic. "Just let me be."

Frank was reading some information on the schedule as they walked toward their train to store their bags. "It says here that riding this train is like taking a trip in a time machine and returning to the great days of rail travel. The carriages are all restored to their old-style luxury. The train has a two-unit diesel-electric locomotive, sightseer lounge car, numerous day coaches, four nineteen-unit sleeping cars, a dining car, a baggage car, and a caboose."

Joe was so busy listening to Frank that he hadn't noticed the person in front of him until he'd stumbled into her.

"Can't you watch where you're going?" a female voice demanded.

Joe stepped back. The woman he'd rammed in to seemed to be in her early twenties. Her eyes were green, and her honey blond hair just touched her shoulders. She wore a green blouse and black jeans. Hanging from her slim neck was a camera fitted with a small telephoto lens. At her feet was a brown suitcase. "Sorry," Joe said.

Frank picked up the girl's case. "Forgive my brother," he said. "He's the family klutz."

The woman glanced from Joe to Frank. Her full lips relaxed into a slight smile. "Your brother?" she said.

"I'm Frank Hardy, and, yes, he's my brother, Joe." Frank nodded toward Andrew Driscoll. "And this is our friend Andrew."

"Pleased to meet you," the young woman replied. "I'm Talia Neiman." She gestured at the platform. "I'm taking the Chicago train. Are you traveling or just meeting someone?"

"We're on the Chicago train, too," Frank said.

"Maybe we'll bump into each other again," Talia said with a grin. "Or maybe—hey, Frank, want to catch a late lunch in the dining car?"

Frank's eyebrows went up. "Sure."

Talia gave him a smile. "Good. Long train trips get so boring without someone to talk to. Shall we say three-fifteen?"

Frank nodded, and Talia set off across the platform and disappeared in the crowd.

"If I knew *that's* what happened on long-distance trips, I'd take the train more often," Andrew said.

"Some people are just born lucky," Frank told him with a grin. "Come on, let's find our compartments."

They were directed to the first sleeping car and quickly found their compartments near the end of the row, by the door. "Here's ours, D," Frank said. Because the train was crowded the boys had to take a large room.

"And here I am in E," Andrew said, sliding open the door to his single-person roomette. "I'm going to wash up, then go buy the things I need."

"And we *are* going along," Frank said.

Surprisingly, the young scientist didn't argue. "Okay," Andrew said. "I'll get you as soon as I'm ready."

Joe nodded. "Good idea."

Frank opened the door and placed his suitcase on a chair. The compartment was roomy and nicely furnished, with one berth made up as a couch, the other hidden in the wall above.

28

Joe tossed his bag on the couch, then sat down beside it.

Picking up a towel, Frank went out into the corridor to wash his face in the lavatory. He filled the basin and splashed cool, refreshing water on his face.

"Beautifying yourself for lunch?" Joe asked Frank as he returned. He was still a little jealous. "She should have asked me. *I'm* the one who bumped into her." He gave his brother an evil smile. "Funny how she looks a little like Callie Shaw."

At the mention of his girlfriend's name Frank's head snapped around. "You know, she does." For a second he felt slightly guilty.

"But don't worry. I won't tell Callie that you go out with strange women whenever her back is turned. You can trust me, Frank." Joe was enjoying teasing his brother.

"It's just lunch," Frank protested.

"Sure. Just think of Callie while you're out enjoying your lunch. And maybe you can spare a thought for Andrew and me, while you're putting pleasure in front of business." Joe started laughing, then stopped as his stomach growled. "I saw a candy machine out by the station entrance," he said. "I know you won't want one, but I think I'll get something. I'll ask Andrew if he wants one."

He stepped from the compartment while Frank was combing his hair. The hallway outside was now filled with passengers, all searching for their compartments. Joe stopped at Andrew's door and knocked. There was no answer.

Maybe he fell asleep and didn't hear me, Joe thought. He knocked louder. Still the younger Driscoll didn't answer. Finally Joe tried the door handle. It was unlocked.

"Andrew?" he called, stepping inside.

The compartment was empty. Joe flicked on the light, searching the place. Andrew hadn't even used it. Slamming the door behind him, Joe headed back to his room.

"What did Andrew say?" Frank asked.

"Nothing. He wasn't there."

Frank was out the door and in the hall like a shot. "Let's check the platform. Looks like he's started his shopping spree without us."

Andrew wasn't on the train platform, but they finally did spot him in the bustling station concourse, carrying his black briefcase, heading for the outside doors. "There he is. Come on."

The Hardys tried to hurry across the station, but it was like trying to move against an army. By the time they reached the sidewalk, Andrew Driscoll was gone.

"What's this guy up to?" Joe wondered out loud as he scanned the area. Everywhere he looked, the sidewalks were jammed with people. The traffic was heavy, too.

30

"I guess we'll find out when he gets back," Frank said.

"If he comes back," Joe growled. He felt angry at Andrew for pulling this stunt. "I'm getting a candy bar. Do we have any other plans until your lunch date?"

"Just to wait for Andrew," Frank said. "I'll stake out the platform. You wait in his compartment. If he sneaks by me, you sit on him, and we'll have a little talk with Mr. Driscoll."

"You got it." Joe boarded the car, heading for Andrew's compartment. Two blond teenage girls in short skirts and with California tans walked by, searching for their compartment. They smiled at Joe, and he almost stopped to chat with them. Instead, he opened Andrew's door and went into the dark room, but he couldn't resist one last look at the girls.

In the light from the hall Joe caught a hint of motion from somewhere to his right side. Could Andrew have returned so soon? And why was it so dark? The shade must be down, he decided in a flash. But before he could turn to check, a loop of wire was slipped around his neck—and pulled tight.

Chapter

4

FOR A SECOND Joe froze, giving his attacker time to drag him backward. When he did swing into action, he whipped his right elbow around and drove it into his attacker's gut. The attacker grunted, and the strangling wire loosened.

Joe threw himself backward, making his attacker stumble. Joe fell over the figure's feet, and the wire slid from Joe's neck.

Pulling free, Joe scrambled to his hands and knees. He saw a dim form in front of him in the darkness, and lashed out with a fist. He missed.

Joe caught a foot in the chest and flopped back, landing heavily. The mysterious attacker didn't strike again, though. Instead, the door flew open and the person darted out. Joe got the impression his attacker was short and thin.

Joe stumbled to his feet and dashed from the compartment. The high school girls were gone, but there were three or four other passengers in the hall. Nearby, a woman was about to enter a compartment. "Excuse me," Joe said.

She paused. "Yes?"

"Did you happen to see anyone come out of here a second ago?"

"I really wasn't paying any attention," the woman admitted. "Sorry I can't help."

"Thanks," Joe said. He rubbed his neck, thankful his attacker hadn't managed to get a firmer grip. His skin was sore but unbroken. Joe headed for the platform, where Frank was checking out the crowd.

Frank's eyes narrowed as he took in the red line across Joe's throat. "What happened?"

"Somebody jumped me with a choke-wire when I went into Andrew's compartment," Joe reported. "I got loose, but the attacker got away. I didn't even get a good look at him. He was short and thin. It might have been one of those guys after the serum—but how did they know we were here?"

"Search me," Frank said. "Did you check the compartment for clues?"

"I came looking for you," Joe said, then

slapped his forehead. "And I left the door open!"

"Come on." Frank led the way back into the sleeping car. He halted in surprise next to Andrew's compartment.

A burly man dressed in a gray suit stood in the doorway, peering inside. He had a ticket in his right hand, and a heavy canvas bag draped over his left shoulder.

Frank strode up to him. "Can we help you?" he demanded, wondering if this was the man who'd jumped his brother.

The man whirled around, his eyes widening. Frank saw that he had thinning dark hair, bushy eyebrows, and a double chin that quivered as he opened his mouth to speak. "I saw the door open, and thought I should check it out."

"Or maybe you were returning to the scene of the crime," Joe cut in angrily.

"Crime?" the man said. "What crime?"

"Somebody attacked me in there a couple of minutes ago," Joe went on. "Maybe it was you."

The man did a double take. "Attack you? Me?" He began laughing. "Why would I do that?"

Joe didn't see what was funny. "Maybe you could tell us."

Realizing that Joe was serious, the man stopped laughing. "I really don't know what you're talking about," he said. "My name is Felix Delray." He extended his right hand. "I'm in the pharmaceutical supply business."

Joe hesitated for a moment, then shook hands.

"I'm in compartment R, down at the other end of this car," Delray went on. "I was on my way there when I saw this door standing open. That's all."

Frank stared at the man. It was a plausible story, and he couldn't accuse the man of something without proof. "Sorry, our mistake," he finally said.

Delray glanced at Joe. "What's this business about someone attacking you?" he asked.

Frank thought quickly. If they weren't careful, Delray might go to the conductor, who could bring in the police. That would mean questions to answer and possibly a missed train. "It's a private matter," he finally said. "Nothing to concern yourself with."

Delray looked from one Hardy to the other. "If you say so." He shrugged and walked away.

Joe glared after the man, but Frank knew what his brother was thinking. "Sorry I got carried away there," Joe said when they entered Andrew's compartment and raised the shade. Nothing was out of place—it was as if Joe had dreamed the fight in there.

Then Joe saw his reflection in the mirror.

The red pressure line on his neck was evidence enough that their enemies played for real.

Joe went down the hall and soaked a washcloth in cold water.

"We've been one step behind these guys all along," Frank complained when his brother returned. "They were onto us even before we got to the labs. They tried to run us off the cliff. Then they had a sniper waiting by Andrew's house."

"They sure don't seem to mind killing people," Joe agreed, setting the cloth on his sore neck.

"I'm not so sure," Frank said, still searching for any clues that Joe's attacker might have left behind. "They didn't use that gun when they ran us off the road. And they had a clear shot at Andrew but used the bullets only to smash his windows. Even with you—"

"Frank, the guy was trying to strangle me."

"Yeah, but you're still here." Frank bent down and peered under the couch.

"You're saying they just want us out of the way, to make their search for the vials easier."

"And when you came in, interrupting their search here, they played a little rough," Frank said. "Maybe the guy even thought you were Andrew. It was dark with the shade down, after all."

"They must figure that Andrew has the

vials." Joe sighed as the cool water soothed his throat. A glance in the mirror showed the red mark was fading.

"Good thing he doesn't," Frank said. He was glad Fenton Hardy had shifted the responsibility of getting the vials to Chicago onto another firm. The guys they were up against were tough.

Joe flopped on the couch and checked his watch. It was almost two-thirty. Where could Andrew be? What if he'd been snatched? And was he being grilled about the vials right now?

Frank gave up searching for clues and sat down on a chair to wait for Andrew. Frank heard someone whistling in the hall. He looked at his watch. It was five of three. The whistler stopped right outside the door. Frank braced himself for an intruder. When the door slid open, though, there stood Andrew Driscoll.

"Hey, guys," he said, swinging a large shopping bag. "What are you doing here?"

"Forget about us." Joe rose to his feet. "Where have you been?"

Andrew hefted the bag. "Buying toothpaste, a toothbrush, a new shirt, stuff like that." He put the bag down on the seat.

"We were supposed to go with you," Frank reminded him.

The younger Driscoll shrugged. "I changed my mind. No hard feelings, I hope?"

Joe was opening his mouth to yell at Andrew

when a shrill whistle pierced the air. The whole room lurched, and they felt a vibration from under the floor. Frank glanced out the window and saw that they were under way.

"Why should I have hard feelings?" Joe asked. "Just because somebody tried to strangle me in your compartment."

Andrew's mouth fell open. "What?"

Joe filled him in. As he spoke, he saw Frank make periodic checks of his watch, and remembered his brother's lunch appointment. "You go on, Frank," he said, finishing up. "I'll take the first watch."

"Watch of what?" Andrew asked warily.

"Watch over you," Joe told him. "From now on, you have two new best friends. We're not letting you out of our sight."

"But how did they know we were here?" Andrew asked, sinking down onto a seat.

"I checked behind us, and never noticed a tail while we rode with Mrs. Lubben," Joe said.

"Maybe the sniper heard us talking on the road," Frank suggested. "Or maybe they had someone covering the train station."

Frank went to the door. "Anyway, lock this behind me," he said. "I won't be long."

Behind him the door was closed with a telltale click. Frank headed for the rear of the train. It took him almost four minutes to travel the length of four sleeping cars.

Frank entered the elegantly furnished dining car. More than a dozen passengers were already sitting at spotless tables that lined both sides of the car. He was delighted to spot Talia sitting halfway down on his left. She beckoned him over.

"You're early, too," Talia joked. "Hungry as I am?"

"Hungrier," Frank said, sitting across from her. Lunch with a pretty girl was a welcome distraction, but still he couldn't get his mind off the attack on Joe. With the bad guys on board, they'd have to spend the trip on constant guard. At least, he—and his dad—had been right. The other side had picked the wrong shell in this game.

"Have you made this trip before?" Talia asked.

Frank glanced up. "What?" He'd been telling himself that he'd have to call Fenton at the first opportunity.

"You seem a little out of it." Talia shook her blond hair so it swung just above her shoulders.

Frank shrugged. "I guess I've got a lot on my mind." He pointed at the camera she still wore around her neck. "Do you take that with you everywhere?"

Talia's high cheekbones went a little pink, but she laughed. "A good photojournalist is never without one."

39

"Are you on assignment?" Frank asked.

"Between assignments, actually," Talia said. "I'll be covering an event in Chicago for *Fashion World* magazine."

Frank was about to ask about her career when he noticed a heavyset figure bearing down on their table.

"Hey, guy, fancy bumping into you." Felix Delray greeted Frank with a big smile. His eyes nearly disappeared behind his chubby cheeks. "Guess it's true what they say about its being a small world."

"Especially on a train, Mr. Delray," Frank said, hoping the man would get the hint and move on.

Instead, Delray sat down at their table. "My pals call me Del," he said. "Mind if I join you? I hate eating alone."

Frank and Talia both knew it was too late to say anything.

"So you're a friend of Frank's?" Talia said.

"Is that his name?" Delray clapped Frank on the shoulder. "We just met a little while ago."

"That's right," Frank said, forcing a smile. "You're in the pharmaceuticals business, aren't you?"

"Best job in the world," Delray told him with a grin. "I scout the country, checking out new drugs that one day might cure all kinds of diseases. When a cure is verified, my company pays out millions of bucks to buy the marketing rights.''

Talia smiled at Frank, her lips silently mouthing the word *boring*.

Delray didn't notice. He was looking at Frank expectantly.

Frank reached for his glass of water, but stopped with it halfway to his lips. Was Delray hinting that he knew about Driscoll's serum?

"Millions of dollars, son," Delray repeated, still staring at Frank. "Think about that."

"Hmph," Frank said, finally taking a sip. I'm thinking all right, he told himself. But right now I'm wondering what's going on.

Chapter
5

"YOUR BROTHER has been gone a long time."
Andrew Driscoll frowned as he glanced at his
watch.

"It's only been twenty minutes," Joe said
from his seat. He glanced up at the scientist,
who had spent most of that time pacing like a
caged tiger. "You're going to wear a groove
in the floor."

"How can you sit there knowing we didn't
shake those guys?" Andrew wrung his hands.
"I bet they've got people all over this train."

"*Or* they might have just one guy," Joe
said. He was surprised at how upset Andrew
was, especially since they were doing their
job. They had successfully distracted the bad
guys from the vials.

"I don't like being cooped up in here," Andrew burst out. "Maybe I'll go for a walk."

"We should stay put until Frank gets back," Joe said. He wished they had some cards. Gin rummy might take Andrew's mind off his problems.

"I can go where I want!" Andrew growled.

"Sure—as long as I tag along." Joe wasn't about to let Andrew disappear again. A light knock sounded on the door. "Who is it?"

"Conductor," a friendly voice said.

Joe opened the door to find a portly man in a gray uniform and cap.

"May I see your ticket, please?" the conductor asked. He turned to Andrew. "Yours, too, sir."

"Sure." Joe reached into his right pants pocket. The ticket wasn't there. He tried his left pocket. No ticket. Where could it be? he wondered. Had he lost it?

"Is something wrong?" the conductor wanted to know.

"I must have left it in my compartment," Joe said, hoping that was the case. "Next door."

"Then we'll go there together and see." The conductor punched Andrew's ticket and motioned for Joe to lead the way.

Hesitating, Joe glanced back at Driscoll. He didn't trust Andrew to stay in his compartment while he was gone. But what could he do? Tie the guy to a chair?

Stepping into the aisle, Joe closed the door behind him. But he couldn't resist one backward glance as he made his way to his compartment. At least Andrew hadn't left immediately after he had.

Joe opened the compartment door. On top of his suitcase lay the ticket. "Here it is," he said, handing it over.

"Thank you, young man," the conductor said. He checked the ticket, punched it, and gave it back. "Have a pleasant trip to Chicago."

"I hope to," Joe said. He pocketed the ticket and quickly took off. He'd been gone about forty-five seconds, which was hardly enough time for Andrew to get anywhere. At least that's what he thought until he saw that the door to Andrew's compartment was slid open a bit.

Stunned, Joe scanned the passageway. Andrew had practically reached the far end and was still moving at a fast trot. What was he up to? Joe started down the corridor, giving chase, darting around the other passengers in the hall.

"What's the rush?" a man called as Joe bumped into him.

Joe didn't answer as he dashed past. Exiting the car, he crossed the platform, and went into the next car. He found at least ten people blocking the passage. Obviously they were all acquainted and traveling together. Several carried cameras.

How was he supposed to get past them? "Excuse me," he called. Even standing on his toes, he couldn't see over or around them. Several people did move aside, but one huge man hadn't budged. "Excuse me, sir," Joe said in his loudest voice.

The man inched closer to the wall. Joe had a clear path now and took off. But where? Andrew Driscoll had vanished. He guessed the scientist was already in the next car.

Ten feet ahead, a thick-bodied man with curly brown hair stepped out from a compartment. He turned toward Joe as he closed his door.

The shock of recognition caused Joe to pull up short. He couldn't believe his eyes. "Curt Loring!" he exclaimed.

Loring was equally shocked. He jumped back, fumbling for the door handle.

In two bounds Joe was at his side. He grabbed the chemist's arm and demanded, "What are you doing here?"

"What's it to you?" Loring blustered.

"How did you know we were on this train?" Joe was determined to get some answers.

"I—I didn't," Loring said.

"Right," Joe snapped. "This is just a big coincidence." A thought jarred him. Could

Loring have been the one who jumped him? No, his attacker was short and thin.

"I don't care what you believe," Loring shook his arm. "Let go of me!"

Joe wanted to keep pushing, but he heard a light cough behind him. "Excuse me. Is there a problem here?"

Pivoting, Joe found an attendant standing behind him. He tensed, figuring Loring would lodge a complaint against him.

"Oh, no problem," Loring said. He slid his door open. "We're old friends."

Then he closed the door in Joe's face. For a second Joe thought about kicking it in, but realized the attendant was still watching him. Maybe it would be better to discuss this with Frank.

With a nod to the elderly man, Joe started walking off. But he'd already noted the compartment—second car, ground floor, F.

At times like this, Joe thought, it was good to have a brother with a mind like Frank's. One who could figure all the angles.

He saw no sign of Andrew Driscoll before he reached the dining car. Scanning the tables, he did spot Frank and Talia Neiman. Who was sitting with them? Joe wondered. Not Felix Delray.

Joe had to hide a grin as he watched his brother's face as Delray babbled on. Talia looked pretty disgusted, too.

"Sorry to bust in like this," Joe said, "but I need to talk with my brother. Now."

Frank actually seemed happy to escape. "Excuse me," he said to Talia.

"Sure," she said, but added quickly, "Can I see you again?"

Frank smiled at Talia. "I'll be in touch. What's your compartment number?"

"Sleeping car three, compartment M," Talia said.

Felix Delray was slurping down a bowl of clam chowder. He stopped to gaze at Frank. "Be seeing you. Just let me know about any cures you stumble across." He laughed at his private joke.

"What was that all about?" Joe asked.

"I wish I knew," Frank said. "When we get in touch with Dad, I'll ask him to run a background check on Delray."

He glanced at his brother. "What are you doing here? Where's Andrew?"

"That's part of the reason I'm here." Joe sighed. "He ran off again."

"How did he get away? I thought you were keeping an eye on him."

Joe explained about the conductor and Andrew's disappearing act. "I was gone about half a minute."

"Great." Frank felt a twinge of guilt. "I should have been there to help."

"I did learn something very interesting

while I was chasing Andrew." Joe leaned closer to whisper to his brother. "Curt Loring is on the train."

"This trip is just full of surprises," Frank said grimly. "Tell me about it on our way back."

"We could visit him on the way," Joe said.

They knocked on the door of his compartment, but there was no answer. Joe pressed his ear to the panel but heard nothing. "Loring may be in there, but I don't feel like breaking down the door to find out."

They went back to their car and headed for their compartment. "We'll need to let Dad know about all this," Frank said. "Our next stop is in Salt Lake City. The train's due in there about eight tomorrow morning. We can call Chicago from there."

Joe was hurrying now to Andrew's compartment. With luck, Andrew would be back there. Joe's hopes crashed when he opened the door to find the compartment empty. He noticed that the contents of Andrew's shopping bag had been scattered all over the couch. Why?

Frank began picking up the items and putting them back in the bag. "Shaving cream, mouthwash, a package of underwear, torn open. Hmm. A magnetic chess and checkers set."

"And a little reading material." Joe scooped a

thin pamphlet that had fallen to the floor. " 'Seven Things Every New Dog Owner Should Know.' " What kind of thing is that to read on a train?"

"Right now, I'm more interested in where Andrew *is* on this train," Frank said. "Could Andrew and Loring be up to something— together?"

"I think he's another person to ask Dad to check out." Joe frowned.

"Him and Delray," Frank said.

"Why was that guy eating with you?"

"He barged up to our table and invited himself." Frank told Joe about the conversation during the meal. "If Delray is in the pharmaceuticals business, I'm a rock star," he finished.

Joe's frown got deeper. "I thought the guy who attacked me was slight, but maybe I was wrong. Maybe Delray or Loring could have been him."

Joe became silent at the sound of faint whistling in the hall. Could it be?

A moment later Andrew Driscoll walked in, a small brown bag in his hand.

"Well, it's the great escape artist," Joe said angrily. "Where did you go this time?"

"I just took a stroll around the train," Andrew said.

Frank was amazed by Andrew's cool act— just like the last time he'd disappeared. The

49

guy seems to be more relaxed now than when I left him, Frank thought. What's he up to?

"Did you know Curt Loring is on this train?" Frank finally said.

Andrew sat down. "No, I didn't. Dad probably mentioned that we'd be taking the train, so Curt tagged along."

Joe sniffed the air. "Hey, what's in the bag?"

"Hamburgers and fries. I figured you might be hungry, so I stopped off for them in the dining car." Andrew smiled. "There's enough to share."

The Hardys stared at each other. One moment Andrew Driscoll was impossible to deal with, the next he was a nice guy. What was going on?

Andrew rummaged around in his shopping bag, coming out with the chess and checkers set. "How about a few games to kill time before we hit the sack?"

"You're on," Frank said with a grin.

Joe stifled a yawn as he stretched out on his bed. He had won the toss and got the couch that folded out. "Too bad we didn't think to bring along some of your electronic gear, like a motion sensor and a beeper. You could have rigged something to Andrew's door."

"When we left Bayport, I didn't expect to

be keeping tabs on a wandering client," Frank said from his bed that pulled out of the wall above Joe. The room had gotten extremely tiny with both beds down.

"But what do we do, take turns standing guard in the corridor?"

Frank gave Joe a look. "Right. I'm sure the attendants and other passengers would love that." He frowned. "We'll just have to take three-hour shifts and check on him every half-hour. We should be able to hear if he tries to leave."

"Do you"—Joe's question was interrupted by a huge yawn—"want the first shift?"

"I think I'd *better* take it. You'll be asleep in ten minutes." Frank lay on top of his berth. In moments he heard Joe snoring softly.

"Don't think about that," he told himself, "or you'll be joining him in dreamland." After the long trip and the shocks of the day, he had to struggle to stay awake. Every thirty minutes, though, he staggered to his feet and checked Andrew's door. It was still locked from the inside.

After three hours he roused Joe and collapsed gratefully into his bed.

It seemed as if he'd barely closed his eyes when a hand was shaking him awake. It couldn't be time already! He felt as if someone had poured lead over his eyelids. Just sitting up took tremendous effort. "Anything happen?" he mumbled.

"Nothing," Joe replied. "It sounds like Andrew's still sawing logs." He flopped down on his bed. "Try to keep the noise down."

"Right. Thanks." Frank's head felt as though it were filled with gray fog. He kept dozing off, then jerking his head back up. Got to stay awake! he told himself. But each time he shuffled out to check on Andrew, it was tougher and tougher to get up.

After the six o'clock check, he lay down in his bed just to rest his eyes for a minute. The rocking of the train had a lulling effect. "I'll close my eyes for just a second," he told himself. "Just a—"

The gray fog went solid black.

Joe heard a loud pounding and jumped out of bed. He saw Frank asleep in his upper berth, then slowly realized someone was at their door. "Coming," he called. A moment later he opened the door.

The conductor stood waiting, a yellow envelope in his hand. "Good morning. Are you Frank or Joe Hardy?"

"I'm Joe." Blinking sleep from his eyes, Joe glanced at his watch. Eight o'clock!

"This is for you," the conductor said. "A messenger just delivered an urgent wire."

"Messenger?" a blurry voice said from

behind Joe. Frank had gotten to his feet and joined his brother in the doorway.

"Yes, sir. We pulled into Salt Lake City forty minutes ago." The conductor smiled and left.

Frank closed the door while Joe fumbled with the envelope. He nearly tore the message inside getting it out.

"It's got to be from Dad," Frank said. "But what's he got to tell us?"

Joe stared in groggy disbelief at the brief message.

Frank and Joe
Andrew has the pea. Call me ASAP.
       Dad

Chapter
6

"WHAT DOES THIS MEAN?" Joe wanted to know.

"Andrew's got the vials." Frank was now fully awake, his face pale. "He's carrying the virus and his father's serum. Remember? We were talking about the shell game—well, Andrew is the shell with the pea."

Joe ran a hand over his face. "Andrew's crazy behavior makes sense now. He must have smuggled the vials out of Starland Lab in that briefcase. Then he ditched us when we got on the train so he could hide them."

"Makes sense," Frank said, nodding. "But what about last night?"

"When he heard that the bad guys were aboard, he got worried. He wanted to check on his stash."

"So he gave us the slip and went to the hiding place." Frank headed for the door. "I think we need to have a little chat with Andrew."

Frank knocked on the door to Andrew's compartment. Andrew didn't answer. Frank then tried the handle, and the door slid open. "Uh-oh."

Joe gasped as he saw the compartment. It was a shambles. Everything that could be moved had been thrown around. Andrew's personal things were scattered everywhere.

"This had to have happened between six and now," Frank said grimly. "I'll start looking for Andrew. You call Dad in Chicago. His number's on the bottom of that wire."

Joe folded the paper and stuck it in his pocket. But as he stepped toward the door, the room shook. A rumble came from under the floor, and they lurched into motion. "We're pulling out of the station!"

The station platform slipped past their window. Frank tried to remember the next stop. Was it Denver, Colorado?

Joe stared with him. "We'll have to wait a while to call Dad," he said.

Frank was staring at the mess still. "If we tell the conductor about this, we'll get tied up with a bunch of questions. I vote we go after Andrew first."

"And I know just the place to start looking." Joe led the way into the hall and clicked the door shut behind him. They went into the next car, to Curt Loring's roomette. Joe banged on the door so hard, the panel shook.

"Who is it?" the familiar voice called out.

"The Hardys," Frank stepped in front of Joe. "Let us in."

"Get lost," Curt Loring snapped.

Joe glanced both ways, making sure no one was in earshot. "Either you open this door, or I'll smash an opening in it."

"Do that, and I'll have you thrown off the train," Loring replied.

"Cool it, Joe," Frank said. He spoke into the door. "Curt, Andrew is missing. Somebody ransacked his compartment. We need your help."

Before the words were out of Frank's mouth, the door was slid open. Curt's face was tight with concern as he stared at them.

"You're not putting me on? Andrew's vanished?" He looked so upset that Joe had to wonder if he was acting.

Frank told the man about what they had found, leaving out the part about Andrew carrying the vials. He saw no sense in letting that secret out, but they could use another pair of eyes to help search the train. "Will you help us find him?"

"Sure," Loring said. "Andrew's my friend."

"I'm glad for that," Joe cut in. "But I still want to know what you're doing here."

"I'm protecting my investment in developing the serum. I have a legitimate interest in the research in Chicago, and I want to be there."

"Did you follow us to the station from Starland Labs?" Joe asked. He'd noticed that Frank had said nothing about the vials and figured why.

"No." Loring became a little embarrassed. "I might as well tell the truth. I listened at Driscoll's door while you made plans."

"I don't like eavesdroppers," Joe said.

"Hey, what else could I do? It's not like the professor was going to tell me anything."

Frank didn't particularly like Loring's story, even if it seemed to make sense. But the man might help find Andrew. And anyway, it would be better to keep him in sight.

"Where do we start looking?" Loring asked.

"Through every car, including the caboose if we need to," Frank said. "Let's do the coaches first."

After searching one coach car, Frank decided they should really find Delray to see if he knew where Andrew was. The trio backtracked to Delray's room and when they didn't find him decided to check the dining car.

"Well, Frank," Talia Neiman said, greeting him cheerily, "just in time for breakfast."

When Frank didn't respond in as cheery a manner, her smile disappeared. "What's wrong? You look like you want to punch someone out."

Could he trust her? Frank wondered. It would help to have one more ally on board. He glanced at his brother, who seemed to read his mind.

"The more, the merrier," Joe muttered.

"We're looking for a friend of ours, Andrew Driscoll," Frank told Talia. "It's important that we find him."

"I was just about to order," Talia said, "but I'd be glad to help if you need it."

Frank still wasn't sure, but Joe took the ball and spoke up. "Great. If we split into teams we can cover the train much faster. You and Talia work toward the back, and Curt and I'll check the coaches and lounge car toward the engine."

Frank remembered his manners. "Oh—Talia Neiman, this is Curt Loring."

"We can all chat later," Joe said. "Let's get started now." He headed back to the door with Curt following.

With a wave, Frank and Talia headed through the dining car, which was packed. The aroma of eggs, bacon, and ham made Frank's mouth water, but he remembered what he was doing and carefully scanned each face at every table.

"Andrew was the other guy with you when your brother bumped into me, right?" Talia asked. When Frank nodded, she added, "I don't think I've ever seen him on the train."

They continued on through corridors crowded with people stretching out their morning kinks.

Frank and Talia made their way back to the eighty-foot baggage car. Standing near the entrance was a thin man dressed like the conductor and with a small hearing aid in his ear.

He glanced at them. "Hi, folks. I'm Assistant Conductor Riley. Can I help? Are you lost?" he said in too loud a voice. Frank wondered if his hearing aid was turned on.

"We're looking for a friend of ours," Frank shouted. "We thought he might be back here."

"Afraid not. The baggage car is kept locked and no one can get in except personnel with keys. A baggage handler puts the baggage on and off at stations."

"I'm sure our friend came back this way," Frank insisted, determined to check out the car. Andrew could easily have forced the lock. "It's really important. See, he's a diabetic and gets a little fuzzy if he misses his medicine."

"But as I said, the door's kept locked," the

assistant conductor repeated, demonstrating by jiggling the handle. He was surprised when it turned in his hand. The door was open. "Well, I'll be— Okay, buddy, you can go in and check, but make it quick."

"Thanks. You can wait here," he said to Talia. Frank moved forward, hurrying down the narrow aisles the mountains of items had created. Maybe Andrew had hidden the vials in the baggage car and was checking on them now?

There were no windows in the dimly lit car, and with the twists and turns the aisles took, Frank could hardly see ten feet ahead of himself. A big crate jutted out on his left. Not until he had inched past it did Frank see the man. He was bent over a rack of suitcases.

"Andrew?" Frank called.

The man straightened up and spun around.

Frank's breath caught in his throat. This wasn't Andrew Driscoll, but he did recognize that hawklike face and cold eyes. This was the tall guy he'd tangled with at Starland Labs! The guy who'd kicked him!

The tall man had gotten over his surprise, and before Frank could move, his hand dipped beneath his jacket. It came out with a pistol— pointed right at Frank's head.

Chapter

7

FRANK STARED down the gun barrel. Its lethal load could be headed straight for his brain any second. Trapped in that narrow aisle, there would be nothing he could do to evade the shot.

At that moment Talia ran up and screamed at the top of her lungs, "Don't shoot!"

The gunman's eyes flicked from Frank to Talia.

That distraction was Frank's only chance, and he took it, lunging for the tall man's wrist. He shoved the gunman's hand up. The automatic discharged, almost deafening them in that confined space. Frank continued the attack by driving his fist into the man's stomach, which doubled him over. He tried to wrestle the automatic pistol from the man's grasp, but his opponent clung to it desperately. Frank continued to hold on to his wrist.

"Be careful!" Talia shouted.

The man came out of his crouched position and swung his arm so violently that Frank was tossed against a pile of crates. Frank did manage to slam the man's gun hand against one of the crates, and the gun clattered to the floor, skittering away.

Frank started after the gun, but the man was too quick and brought his knee up into the pit of Frank's stomach. Frank lost his breath in a *whooof!* of agony and flopped back, dazed, against a wall of crates. The man pushed past Talia toward the front of the car.

"Frank!" Talia leapt forward and took his arm.

The tall man was escaping! Frank tottered forward to chase him, but Talia wasn't letting go of him. He reeled as she pulled him back. Either she's got a grip like iron, he thought woozily, or I'm worse off than I think. "Got to—follow," he said.

"Are you nuts?" Talia hissed. "In your condition? That guy will kill you!"

"Can take care of myself," Frank gasped.

Shaking her head, Talia let go of his arm. Frank got about two feet down the aisle before he collided with the assistant conductor.

"What's going on back here?" the assistant conductor demanded. "Some clown nearly knocked me down just now."

"We were attacked," Frank answered, remembering that the man didn't hear very well and probably hadn't even heard the shot. "That man tried to shoot me." He gave up on trying to chase the guy. By now, he'd be well hidden.

"Is that a gun?" Mr. Riley asked, pointing to the floor. Still lying there was a 9-mm automatic. The man knelt to reach for it, but Frank dropped to his knees and pushed his hand away.

"You've got a pen in your shirt pocket," Frank shouted. "Slip it into the barrel and pick it up that way. We want to save any fingerprints."

The man did as he was told, staring at Frank's mouth the whole time.

Frank stepped past Riley, eager to warn Joe about the tall man being on the train.

"I'll have to report this to my boss, the conductor." The man's words stopped him.

"Of course. I'm Frank Hardy. I'm in the first sleeping car, room D, if he wants to speak with me."

"I can guarantee he will." Mr. Riley turned to face Talia directly. "What about you, young lady?"

"Talia Neiman. Third sleeping car, room M."

"Fine. Please go to your compartments and wait there."

The man led the way out of the baggage car, followed by Talia, then Frank. Talia glanced at him as they crossed to the next car. "I'm sorry about holding you back," she said, "but you looked pretty wiped out. If that guy had gotten his hands on you—well, I was afraid for you."

"Forget it." Frank was annoyed that the guy had gotten away, but the fact that Talia was worried about him tugged a half-smile onto his face.

They walked in silence until they reached Talia's compartment. "Keep your door locked until the conductor comes," Frank said.

Talia froze in the doorway, staring at him. "You think I'm in danger?"

"That guy has a problem with me, not you, but I don't want to take any chances."

"You know a lot more about this than you're telling me," Talia said bluntly. "What's going on?"

"I'll try to fill you in later, but right now I want to find my brother." He waved goodbye, then started back along the train. As he entered his own car he saw Joe and Curt Loring approaching.

"We went all the way to the lounge car,"

Joe reported. "And found zilch. How about you?"

"I think I found the guy who tried to choke you in our compartment yesterday," Frank said. "The same guy who nailed me at the lab—he's on board."

He went on to tell Joe and Curt about what happened when he searched the baggage car. Joe's face was tense and his fists were clenched. Oddly, Frank noticed, Loring had begun to sweat. "That's about it. I promised to wait in our compartment until the conductor shows up."

Loring cleared his throat. "Unless you guys really need me, I'd like to go."

"Suit yourself." Joe shrugged. He stared at the man's back. "Some help he was," he muttered to Frank. "Hardly said a single word during the search."

"A search that didn't turn up Andrew." Frank hoped that the tall man hadn't caught up with the younger Driscoll. "I hope he's okay."

Behind him, Joe had stopped beside a compartment door. It was open just a crack, and he could just make out someone crouching inside. Joe pushed against the door. "If you're so eager to hear what we're saying, why don't you come out?"

The door slid open against Joe's push, scaring the person inside and knocking him off balance. Frank walked back to join Joe and an embarrassed Felix Delray on the floor of his roomette. He noticed Delray was wearing the same gray suit he'd had on the day before, now badly rumpled. The guy must have slept in it, he thought. Then he remembered that he'd done exactly the same thing.

"Hello again." Delray grunted as he pulled himself to his feet. "I didn't know you guys were—"

"No?" Joe cut in. "Do you always stay in your room with the door ajar, listening in on other people's conversations?"

Delray bristled. "What are you saying? I just hadn't closed my door all the way."

"Why don't I believe you?" Joe squared off against Delray.

Frank grabbed his brother's arm. "Come on. The conductor will be waiting for us."

"I don't like eavesdroppers," Joe growled. "If he sticks his nose in our business—"

"Are you threatening me?" Delray raised his voice, so anyone in the corridor would hear.

He's doing it on purpose, Frank realized, poking his head out the door to check for other passengers. A couple of people were staring at him. With witnesses around, he figures Joe won't dare try anything.

Joe followed Frank down to Andrew's compartment. "Let's just check to see if he's back," Frank said. Inside, the place was still a mess—and still empty.

Frank then opened the door to their compartment and froze in the entrance. It looked as if the same tornado that had wrecked Andrew's room had passed through theirs as well.

Their clothes and belongings were strewn everywhere. Frank saw a sweater of his that had been torn apart.

Joe was furious, his fists bunched at his sides. "This stinks!"

"Actually, it's good news," Frank said.

Joe stared at his brother. "Did you get thrown on your head during that fight in the baggage car?"

"No, this *is* good news." Frank pointed at the mess. "If the bad guys are still searching, it means they haven't found the vials yet."

"So we're not the only ones who don't have a clue."

Frank grinned at his brother. "But at least Andrew's on our side," he reminded Joe.

He bent to scoop up some of his clothes and caught a glimpse of something in the tiny closet in the corner. Frank shifted a little, trying to see better. He wasn't crazy. There was a human finger propped against the door edge.

Signaling for Joe to be quiet, Frank stepped

noiselessly to the door. With luck, they would capture the guy who ransacked their room. He grabbed the door handle and jerked the door open.

Out of the closet toppled the body of Andrew Driscoll!

Chapter

8

FRANK AND JOE HARDY stood frozen as Andrew fell to the floor.

There was no doubt that Andrew was dead. Looped under his contorted face was a length of black wire. Still, Joe dropped to one knee to feel for a pulse. "I was just beginning to like him," he whispered. "Now he's—gone. This is going to kill Professor Driscoll. Imagine sending your son off on a mission and having him die."

"Why did he have to sneak off that one last time?" Frank said. "Why couldn't he just have trusted us?" He headed for the door. "We've got to report this right away. I'll go find the conductor. You stay with the—with Andrew."

Frank paused for a second in the doorway. "And keep the door locked until I get back." He didn't want to think how *their* father would react to the death of a son.

Joe locked the door, leaning against it. Then he stared down at the body of Andrew Driscoll. Would the tall man from Starland have had time enough to kill Andrew? The body was still slightly warm, so Joe guessed he would have had. That didn't necessarily mean he was the killer, only that he could be. Had it been done in their compartment, or somewhere else? If it happened elsewhere, how had the killer gotten the body to their compartment without being seen?

Maybe Andrew had something on him that could lead Joe and Frank to where the vials were hidden. Joe drew a deep breath, then dropped to his knees to search the young scientist's pockets. He found spare change, forty dollars in cash, a folder with a couple of credit cards, a comb, and several sticks of chewing gum.

In a rear pocket, he discovered three small biscuits shaped like bones—one green, one yellow, one red. They looked like doggie treats. I guess he must have a pet at home, Joe thought. Poor pooch. He returned his finds to the appropriate pockets.

Joe found the chair and tried to watch the scenery outside, but his eyes kept returning to Andrew. He or Frank could just as easily have wound up there. A little chill ran down his spine. They still could.

Frank had almost reached the end of the car when he saw the conductor enter. The man appeared upset. Frank halted. "I believe you're looking for me."

The portly man stopped. "You're Frank Hardy?" Before Frank could even answer, the conductor went on. "I'm Conductor Herman. I was just told a crazy story about a fight. Did someone really shoot at you?"

"It's a long story." Frank led the conductor to the platform between cars so they could have some privacy. He was weighing the risks of revealing the full situation, including the vials. Was it worth creating a panic over a killer virus hidden aboard? He had to consult with his father first. Finally he told an edited version.

The conductor shook his head. "You realize I'll have to report this."

Frank sighed. "I'm afraid that's not all you'll have to report." He leaned closer to the conductor. "There's been a murder."

The man jumped as if he'd just touched a live wire. Then he drew himself up, glaring at Frank. "Is this a setup for some stupid joke?"

"I only wish it was," Frank said. "Come

to our compartment and see for yourself.'' He led the way and knocked. ''Joe, I'm back.''

Joe opened the door, then had to step back as Mr. Herman pushed his way in. Frank followed, closing the door quickly so passersby wouldn't see the body.

A hiss of indrawn breath came from the conductor as he stared at Andrew Driscoll. He fell to one knee, checking for vital signs. ''Dead,'' he muttered. ''Murdered,'' he added, staring at the loop of wire around the neck.

The man got unsteadily to his feet. ''They train us how to handle dead bodies,'' he said, in a hushed voice. ''People die on railroads, just like anywhere. I've seen heart attacks, strokes, accidents. But this is the first killing I ever came across.''

He pulled himself together, staring at the boys. ''Do you know the name of the deceased?''

''Andrew Driscoll,'' Frank replied. ''He was traveling to Chicago with us. And he may have been killed by the same man who shot at me.'' He sighed. If I had caught that guy in the baggage car, maybe this wouldn't have happened.

The conductor asked a few more questions, getting the Hardys' names and finding out the last time they'd seen Andrew. He wrote the answers on a notepad, flipped it shut, and put it in his pocket. ''I'm sure you know this is a matter for the police. I'll have the engineer radio ahead and alert the dispatcher at our next stop. That'll be Denver. The authorities there will have the facilities to get to the bottom of this."

"Do you want us to stay here?" Joe asked.

"Yes," Mr. Herman answered, then shook his head. "No. This is a crime scene. The police will want to check for fingerprints, that sort of thing. We'll leave your compartment just as it is."

He took a deep breath. "There's an empty compartment in the next car. Move in there."

The boys moved out, and the conductor locked the door. "I'd advise you two to keep a low profile until we get to Denver," the man said.

"How long will that be?" Joe asked.

"Not till after nightfall," the conductor replied. "Getting over the Rocky Mountains isn't a straight run. We have to deal with a lot of curves and steep grades."

He led the Hardys to their new compartment. "I'm going to talk to the engineer now. Then I'll be back with some more questions. Please try to stay out of trouble."

Joe flopped onto the new couch. "So now what? I'd say we were at a dead end."

Frank shook his head. "For once, the bad guys aren't ahead of us. If they had the vials, they wouldn't have bothered searching our compartment. No, Andrew hid them safely—somewhere on this train."

Joe groaned. "Then we'll have to search it again, from engine to caboose."

Frank rose to his feet. "I suppose we should tell Loring the news. Besides, he might be able to help us search."

As he headed toward Curt Loring's compartment, Frank's face was grim. He didn't like the idea of a deadly virus just lying around in a glass tube on the train. What if someone who didn't know any better found the vial and opened it? They could easily kill everyone on the train!

He knocked a little more sharply than usual on Loring's door. No answer.

"Is he hiding out, or just gone?" Joe wondered.

"There's only one way to find out." Frank tried the handle, and the door slid open to reveal an all-too-familiar scene. "Another happy customer of the Acme Searching and Wrecking Crew," Frank said as he took in the mess.

Joe headed straight for the closet and opened it. "Loring isn't there, at least. He might be alive and hiding somewhere."

"Let's get to work," Frank said. "It's probably a waste of time, but there may be a clue here." He bent down and started poking through clothes and possessions. Just as he was about to straighten up, he noticed a piece of paper sticking out from a sock, which was tossed on the back of a chair. "What's this?"

Frank pulled the paper loose. It was a phone number with a 415 area code. "That's San Francisco. I remember calling Dad out there recently."

"You think it means something?" Joe asked.

Frank shrugged. "Since it was hidden in Loring's sock it probably means he wanted it kept safe. It obviously wasn't found by whoever tossed this room. I'll give it to Dad to run it down."

"Now let's see if we can run Loring down, or those vials." Joe opened the compartment door. "You know, the guys we're up against seem very well informed. How did they know Loring was aboard—or even that Loring worked on the professor's research?"

"Bugs in the lab? A spy? Mind readers?" Frank shrugged. "Take your pick. But they do seem to know everything about our clients and us."

"We'll get a shot at them," Joe predicted confidently.

They made it as far forward as the lounge car, which had only a couple of people in it since it was still early. It had both an upper and lower level, like a double-decker bus. Stairs led to the upper level, where large wrap-around picture windows allowed passengers to enjoy the view.

Joe was almost at the steps when a tall man in a brown suit appeared on the top stair and came down three steps. Joe paused, thinking there was something familiar about the guy.

The man glared down at him, and a mental picture suddenly clicked in Joe's brain. It was the hawk-faced guy from Starland, the one who'd nearly killed Frank and the one who might have killed Andrew.

Just then he heard his brother yell a warning. "Joe! Look out! He's the one!"

Hawk-face retreated a step, but Joe charged up a couple of stairs, lunging for his legs. He missed. If I can yank his feet out from under him, we'll have this guy, he thought. Frank took his gun, so he's got to be unarmed.

The man's hand then moved to his pocket. Joe felt a chill. Or is he?

But his hand seemed to be empty when it came back out. Joe climbed another step.

Suddenly Hawk-face flicked his wrist, and a four-inch metal blade clicked into place. His hand came down, a switchblade gleaming as it slashed toward Joe's face.

Chapter
9

ACTING ON PURE REFLEX, Joe hurled himself to the right, the blade missing his eye by an inch. He toppled down the stairs.

Frank went up the stairs after the man then. The knife flew at his stomach. Frank threw himself against the stair rail as the blade just missed his belt buckle.

Off balance, Frank promised himself not to let the guy get away and lurched forward to grab the man's ankles. One yank and the thug had twisted and fallen flat onto his stomach. Backpedaling, Frank dragged him down the stairs.

The man tried to twist round, the knife still in his hand, but Joe joined the fight and pinned the man's wrist with his foot. Joe bent over, lifted the guy's head, and sent a fist right to the point of his chin. "Out like a light," he declared, scooping up the knife in his handkerchief.

"Fine. Take an arm," Frank said. He took the left, Joe the right, and they lifted their sagging attacker upright.

Two male passengers barred their way. "What do you think you're doing?" one demanded.

"I think we're capturing a murderer," Frank told the man. "Why don't you get the conductor?" He smiled grimly as the man raced away.

If this guy turns out to be the killer, it will make our search for the vials a lot easier, Frank thought. At least we won't be looking over our shoulders all the time. He stopped suddenly. Unless he has the vials already.

"Joe," he said, "hold him up."

With Joe keeping the man erect, Frank went through the attacker's pockets. He found a two-inch-thick wad of twenty-dollar bills, which he quickly replaced. There was also a wallet, with a New York State driver's license. The photo ID identified the man as Robert Steiner. Frank put the wallet back.

A commotion at the end of the car made him turn. The conductor and an attendant were rushing toward them. "Here comes the cavalry," Frank said.

Mr. Herman's face was almost purple with rage as he came up to Frank. "I thought I told you—"

"We have a present for you," Frank announced. "This is the guy who shot at me."

"Here's the knife he was slashing at us with. What do we do with it—and him?" Joe asked the conductor, who was staring pop-eyed.

"Good question," the trainman finally said, staring at the knife. "I don't have the authority to arrest anyone, but legally I am in charge of this train. I can take whatever steps are necessary to protect the passengers."

Frank heard murmuring from behind the conductor. A small audience of passengers had gathered.

"We'll tie him up and put him in a compartment until we reach Denver," the conductor decided. "Then the police can handle it."

"Fine," Joe said. "Just show us where you want him."

"No, no. You two have done enough already," the conductor said. "I'll get some of my men to help." The conductor took off his sweater vest and wrapped the knife in it. Then he gestured for an assistant conductor and an attendant to help with the prisoner. Turning to the excited crowd behind him, he said, "Ladies and gentlemen, there's no cause for alarm. Everything is under control. Please

79

go back to your seats and enjoy the trip."
He whispered to his men, "Come on—get him
out."

Joe leaned over to Frank. "The search goes
on?' he said softly.

Frank nodded. "We'll work our way back
from here. The idea is to check every public
part of the train—rest rooms and all."

"What about going from compartment to
compartment?" Joe asked.

"I don't think the conductor would stand
for us disturbing his passengers. And I'm not
sure I'd like to tell him why we needed to do
it." Frank frowned, trying to put himself in
Andrew Driscoll's shoes. Where would be the
safest spot to hide a pair of potentially dangerous vials?

"Well, don't just stand there," Joe said.
"Start looking!"

They started the search eagerly. But their
enthusiasm dwindled after hours of not finding
either the vials or Curt Loring. They glanced
under seats for a glimpse of Andrew's black
briefcase. They got curious looks from passengers as they poked into various nooks and
crannies. Once an attendant caught them rum-
maging through a utility closet and shooed
them away.

It was almost sunset by now, and as he
trailed his brother, Joe was ready to admit

defeat. "All that's left is the baggage car," he said, "unless you count the caboose."

Frank just rubbed his eyes. He'd had hardly any sleep for the past forty-eight hours, and it was catching up with him. Tiredly they tried the handle on the baggage car. It was locked, and Frank wasn't sure he had the energy to pick the lock right then. He was worn out and at least needed something to eat.

"Now what?" Joe wanted to know.

"How about a hot meal?" Frank suggested, and he led them to the dining car. Joe ordered a cheeseburger, while Frank had fried chicken. Depressed, they ate quickly and silently.

"We'll be in Denver soon. Might as well wash up and wait for the police," Frank said when they were done.

"Do we tell them about the vials?" Joe asked.

Frank shook his head. "We tell no one until we've talked to Dad. We just wait for the cops and try not to make them suspicious." He led the way to their new compartment and opened the door. "I'll wash up first," he said, heading for the lavatory.

Joe sat, staring out the window at sunset in the Rockies. The sun had almost disappeared behind craggy peaks. He chuckled to himself. Imagine going through some of the greatest scenery on earth and missing it so I could search bathrooms, he thought.

Frank finished up, and Joe went out and took his place to wash up. Sitting by the window, Frank dozed until he heard the train's whistle announce their arrival in Denver. Buildings flashed by, and soon they were pulling into Union Station. Frank had to get to a phone before he talked to the police.

In moments, though, there was a knock on the door. Frank answered, only to find the conductor with a thin, sad-faced man in a dark green suit under a down jacket. The stranger extended his arm, displaying a badge.

"This is Captain Al Simmonds of the Denver police. Captain, meet Frank and Joe Hardy."

Simmonds entered. "Thank you, Mr. Herman. That'll be all." He closed the door, shook the boys' hands, and gestured to the seat.

"Do you want us to show you the body?" Joe asked.

"A crime scene crew is already with Andrew Driscoll," Simmonds said. "But I understand you two knew the deceased. What can you tell me about him?"

For the better part of the next hour, they talked about Andrew, what he'd done on the train, and what had happened to them. The captain leaned back, closing the notepad he'd frequently scribbled in. His face was even sadder than it had been at first. "Well, you've been very cooperative. But I still don't understand what the gunman was after. What motive could he possibly have for strangling Driscoll?"

Joe glanced at Frank. Neither of them had mentioned a word about the vials of virus and serum. They still kept quiet.

"Maybe it was a simple robbery," Simmonds went on, rising. "The conductor has already turned over the pistol and the knife to us."

Frank leaned forward. "Do you mind if we call our dad now?"

"Go ahead," Simmonds said.

The Hardys were out of the room and on the platform in a flash. There were people everywhere. Joe spotted a bank of telephones against a far wall and rushed toward them, pulling the wire from his pocket.

"I have change," Frank said, slipping into the booth. He took the wire, dialed the number for the Lakeshore Grand, and asked for his father's room.

"Hello?" Fenton Hardy came on the line.

"Dad, it's us—with very sad news." Frank went on to give the whole story, leaving nothing out. He told about Loring being aboard and gave his father the San Francisco telephone number they'd found in Loring's room. Frank also requested a background check on

Felix Delray. Finally he concluded with "What do you want us to do?"

"Stay on the train. I guess I'd have to advise you to keep quiet about the vials, but, Frank, you've got to find them." Fenton sighed. "I'll break the news about Andrew to the professor. He's due here any minute."

"Would he know where Andrew hid the vials?" Frank asked hopefully.

"No. He says he gave Andrew complete freedom of action when he gave him the vials."

"Why'd he send the vials with Andrew rather than trust the security firm you hired?"

"What can I say? The professor doesn't trust strangers," Fenton explained. "He gave the real vials to Andrew, and phonies to the security firm. Apparently, he figured we'd be the primary target and that no one would go after the three of you. I didn't know until we got here. Sorry to put you in the middle of this." He paused. "I'll check with friends on the Denver force to see if I can learn anything else. Take care and be extra careful."

"So long, Dad." Frank hung up the phone.

"That's it, then?" Joe shoved his hands in his pockets. "Nothing from the professor about where Andrew could have hidden the vials?" Frank shook his head. Joe suddenly stood up straight and stiffened as they made their way back to their car. "Hey, Frank! Look."

Frank stared down the track to watch as two men unloaded a long wooden crate from the baggage car. "That would be big enough to conceal a body," he said thoughtfully.

Joe nodded. "I was thinking the same thing. Do you think Loring's in there?"

"It's a long shot," Frank objected.

"Can we afford not to check?" Joe asked.

Frank hesitated for a moment. "No," he finally said.

That was all Joe needed to hear. He started back for the baggage car, but cutting through the crowd on the platform was like fighting the tide. The platform was the first in a long line and was built up against an outside wall. By the time the Hardys reached the car, the men had taken the crate out a side exit. They burst through the same doors into the dark night and saw a van pulling away. Under a streetlight, Joe could see the driver and recognized him as one of the men who'd done the moving. "What do we do now?" he asked.

Frank had run into the street, waving frantically to a cab, "Taxi!"

The driver stared a little suspiciously at the boys. They were probably the only people in Denver without coats on. "What's the problem, Chief?" he finally asked.

Frank pointed down the street to the set of red taillights. "Follow that van!"

The cabbie stared at him for a second. "You're joking, right?"

"This is no joke," Joe said, joining Frank in the cab. "We can't lose that van. It's important, and it's for real."

The driver put the car in gear. "Okay, but don't expect any stunt driving. No fare is worth a ticket."

As the cab gave chase, Joe followed the street signs. They trailed the van southeast on Sixteenth Street, into the skyscraper-dominated heart of downtown Denver. After five minutes the van took a left onto Glenarm Place. Joe's voice was high as he yelled, "There he goes!" The van had turned into an alley.

"I see it," the cabbie replied. "Keep your shirt on." Two minutes later he pulled into the same alley and promptly braked.

The van was parked twenty yards away, and the men were just taking the crate through the rear door of a building.

"Wait here for us," Frank said, hopping out and hoping they didn't freeze.

"Hey, what about my fare?" the cabbie yelled, but the Hardys were already going inside.

Joe had pushed on the door before it latched, and they had stepped into a short, dark hallway. Beyond a half-open door, outlined with light, they could hear a man's voice. "I didn't think we could pull this off. But they're here, and they're going to make us a mint!"

Joe glanced at Frank. It had to mean that the vials—and maybe Loring's body—were behind that door!

A good shove sent the door open all the way. Joe leapt forward into a strongly scented room. Two men stood over the crate.

One whirled around, a crowbar in his hand, snarling, "What do *you* want?"

Chapter

10

JOE STOOD FROZEN, staring—not at the crowbar but at the rest of the room. Glass refrigerated containers lined the walls. They were filled with violent splashes of colorful flowers—roses, tulips, brilliant tropical buds Joe couldn't even identify.

The man with the bar hadn't moved to attack. Nor had his partner, nor had the young woman in the apron Joe now noticed behind them. They stood in a protective group around the crate, and the vivid purple flowers it contained.

"Look, kid," the man with the crowbar said, "I don't know what your problem is, but we've got flowers to unload. So tell us—what do you want?"

Joe was too embarrassed to speak. He could feel his face turning as red as the case of roses at his elbow.

Frank stepped through the door and came to his rescue. "Sorry for bursting in. Did you see a small dog run in here?"

The man with the crowbar shook his head. "If your pooch ran away, he didn't come in here."

"Thanks," Frank said. "Come on, Joe, let's keep looking."

Joe pasted a smile on his face and escaped as quickly as possible. The brothers were silent all the way back to Union Station, feeling like complete idiots. After paying the taxi fare, they made their way inside to the waiting area. Their hour-and-a-half layover was almost over, and soon they'd be on the move again.

"Hey, Hardys!" a voice shouted from behind them. They turned to see Felix Delray waddling their way. He was carrying an overnight bag and wore a blue down jacket and blue slacks with a knife-edge crease that gave them away as being brand-new.

"I was looking for you guys," Delray said.

"We went out."

Joe smiled. Frank obviously wasn't going to tell him anything.

"Me, too," Delray said. "Hear about the murder on board?" He watched their faces avidly.

"We know about it." Frank couldn't disguise the dislike he was feeling for Delray.

Delray wouldn't be shook off, though. "Someone told me the dead man was Andrew Driscoll. You knew him, right?"

Joe stared. What was it with this guy?

"Come on, is it true?" Delray pressed.

Joe had had enough. "I don't know where you come off, grilling us like this."

"Hey, I was just curious. I wondered if it had anything to do with that fight you two had in the lounge car." Delray stared eagerly at him.

Joe stared back. "How did you hear about that?"

"Are you kidding? You guys are the talk of the train." Delray laughed. "So why don't you give me the real lowdown?"

"Let's not and pretend we did," Frank cut in coldly. They were about to walk off when they saw two men in white wheeling a gurney away from their train. On the gurney was a body bag. A crowd had gathered and was slowly following behind.

"There goes Driscoll now," Delray said. "They say the poor slob was strangled."

Joe whipped around. "Andrew wasn't a slob."

Delray grinned in triumph. "So you *did* know him, huh? Why wouldn't you admit it?"

Frank grabbed his brother's arm before Joe

hit the man. He also gave Delray a long look. "You know, the police might be interested in someone with so many questions about the murder. Maybe they can fill you in, and at the same time ask you a few things."

"The police?" Delray stiffened. "Hey, there's no need to involve them. I was just making conversation."

"Then go make it someplace else," Joe told him bluntly.

Hefting his overnight bag, Delray hurried off.

"What *is* it about that bozo?" Joe wondered.

"There's more to him than pharmaceuticals," Frank agreed. "Maybe we'll get to the bottom of it before we reach Chicago."

Joe stared after the gurney. We'd better get this solved by then, he thought. This case has already cost one human life too many.

"Frank—Joe, I'm sorry about your friend." Talia Neiman had come up and was standing beside them. "Why would anyone do something like this?"

Frank stared off in silence. Both Hardys knew the answer to Talia's question, but they couldn't tell her. They just stood, watching the gurney being wheeled through a glass door to a lit up ambulance outside. At least the cops have the guy who did it, Joe thought. It's not much, but it's something.

Talia fiddled with her camera, then glanced

91

at the train. "I don't want to be alone right now. Would you join me for a late dinner in the dining car after we get moving again?" She turned to Joe. "Both of you?"

"You want me to come?" Joe said.

She managed a smile. "Misery loves lots of company. What do you say, guys?"

Frank hesitated. Any delay meant time lost in searching for the vials. Still, they were both hungry and it would be rude to brush Talia off.

Joe stepped in. "Sure, no problem."

Talia's smile warmed. "Great. We'll meet in the dining car at eight-fifteen." With a wave, she headed for the train.

"She's not such a bad person," Joe said, giving Frank a sidelong glance. "Although her taste in men leaves a lot to be desired."

"Hah! You're just jealous!" Frank and Joe had made their way to their car and were just stepping up to climb on board when a sharp voice called to them from the platform.

"Hold up there, gentlemen."

Joe tensed, recognizing the voice before he turned. Captain Al Simmonds had his hands in his pockets and a friendly grin on his lips.

"I've been hearing about you on the phone," the police detective said. "From an investigator named Fenton Hardy."

"Dad?" Joe said in surprise.

The captain nodded. "He telephoned headquarters from Chicago and wanted to speak to the officer in charge of the Driscoll case. The word was radioed to one of our cars out front, then relayed to me. So I got on the horn, long distance."

"Did he explain everything to you?" Frank asked.

"He told me enough—that you're working on a case with heavy government ties." Simmonds's eyes grew sharp. "He also asked me to give you all the cooperation I could. I said fine."

Joe sighed with relief. Trust Dad to pull the right strings.

"Your father asked me to pass on some hot news. There was an attempt to kidnap Andrew Driscoll's father a little while ago."

Frank's jaw dropped. *"What?"*

"Apparently two guys tried to take him off the street right in front of the hotel. Driscoll put up a fight, and some officers on patrol saw what was going on. They've got the two mugs in custody, but so far the guys aren't talking. Your dad says one of them was Steiner's assistant in San Francisco."

The attack was bad news, but it did mean that the other side still hadn't gotten the vials.

"Interestingly, our own Mr. Steiner or whoever is doing a pretty good clam impersonation," Simmonds went on. "We haven't gotten anything out of him."

"Too bad." Joe frowned. "What do you mean, 'Steiner or whoever'?"

"That New York driver's license is a phony," Simmonds said. "We checked with the Department of Motor Vehicles there, and they have no record of that license being issued to a Robert Steiner."

Frank sighed. Whoever they were up against, they were pros—and didn't miss a trick.

"The crime scene boys are done, but I'm leaving one of my men, Sergeant Yankton, aboard for follow-up. He'll travel with you to the next stop, checking with passengers and asking what they might have seen. He's under orders to assist you in any way possible."

"Thanks," Frank said.

But Captain Simmonds looked troubled. "There's one more thing—and you won't like it."

Frank and Joe were nervous as they waited.

"We searched the phony Steiner's compartment, finding another knife and, believe it or not, a sawed-off shotgun. But no strangling wires."

"He left it around Andrew's neck," Joe said grimly.

The officer shook his head. "No. This guy didn't strangle Driscoll. He *couldn't.*"

Both Hardys stared in disbelief.

"When we examined 'Steiner,' we found his left hand is almost paralyzed—old nerve damage." Simmonds shook his head. "You need two hands to strangle someone with a wire. This guy was one hand short."

Joe blinked, almost dazed. "But if Steiner didn't kill Andrew—"

Frank finished grimly. "Who *did?*"

FIVE MINUTES LATER the train pulled out

Chapter

11

FIVE MINUTES LATER the train pulled out from Union Station. Joe felt the car jerk to a start as he sat staring at his own reflection in the dark glass. Through the window he could soon see the night lights of Denver speeding by. "So what's next?" he asked his brother.

"I'm stumped," Frank admitted. He was walking back and forth, deep in thought. There must be a way to recover the vials, he reasoned. And there was still a killer to be caught. But no matter how hard he racked his brain, he came up blank.

"We could search the train again," Joe suggested. "Not that it would do any good."

"I agree," Frank conceded. "No, we need to come up with clues. Let's check out Loring's compartment on the way to the dining car.''

Joe was out of the chair in a flash. He'd rather do anything than sit around feeling useless. ''And if we bump into Delray, let's give him the third degree.'' He stepped into the passageway and nearly collided with the two teenage girls he'd seen before. They had to step back to avoid being run over.

One was blond, the other blonder still. ''Hi, there.'' The platinum one gave him a big smile. ''What's your hurry?''

''Yeah,'' her darker-haired friend added. ''Every time we see you, you're in a rush.''

''Sorry,'' Joe said. ''I should have looked before I barged out.''

''I'm Ruth,'' the blonder girl said. Then she pointed to her companion. ''This is Sally, my best friend. My mom is taking us to Omaha to visit her sister. She just had a baby.''

''Your mom?'' Joe said.

Both girls giggled. Ruth shook her head and said, ''No, silly. My mom's sister.''

Frank stepped into the doorway. He was about to remind his brother that they had business to attend to when he froze, startled.

He caught sight of Curt Loring peeking in the door between cars. He saw Frank and started to enter.

''Joe,'' Frank said softly.

Glancing around, Joe saw his brother's

expression and gazed in the same direction. He was dumbfounded to see Loring. The scientist seemed to stare past them and then fled as if in panic.

"After him!" Frank said. They both took several strides. Unexpectedly, someone shouted behind them just then.

"Frank and Joe Hardy!"

Frank paused and whirled around, his brother doing the same, and saw a middle-aged man in a blue suit approaching at a slow jog.

"You are Frank and Joe Hardy, aren't you?" the man asked. He had short, sandy hair and brown eyes.

"That's right." Joe was desperate to take off after the scientist and almost bolted, but didn't because the man had produced a badge.

"I'm Sergeant Yankton. Captain Simmonds told me to lend you guys a hand if—"

"We need a hand now, Sergeant," Frank interrupted urgently. "We just saw a man who might know about Andrew Driscoll's death."

"Where?" the police officer asked in surprise.

"Follow us," Frank said, dashing to the door. He yanked it open and raced through the two cars of coach seats to the lounge car. No one resembling Loring was in either car.

Frank went through the lounge car before he had to halt in utter confusion. Loring was nowhere in sight. Upstairs. He figured the scientist had to go up there and so he dashed to the steps. But when he reached the upper level he saw only unfamiliar faces.

"Where did he go?" Joe asked, frustrated, a step behind his brother. Through the picture windows he saw only stars and the dark Colorado sky.

"Mind telling me who we're after?" Sergeant Yankton asked, a little out of breath.

Frank saw no reason to keep it a secret. "A man named Curt Loring. He worked with Andrew Driscoll at the Starland Research Facility in California."

"Loring, huh?" The police officer reached into his jacket pocket and pulled out a notepad, then wrote the name down.

Frank frowned in puzzlement. Why had Loring run off like that? Could he have spotted the officer? But why was he afraid of the police? How would he even know Yankton was the police? Frank suddenly remembered Talia and said, "We're supposed to meet someone in the dining car. Care to tag along?"

"I could use a cup of coffee," Yankton said. He turned and followed the Hardys. "Is it true your father is Fenton Hardy?"

"Yes. Do you know him?" Joe responded.

"Not personally. But I've heard of him. They say he's one of the best," Yankton said.

Joe smiled. "He is. He's taught us everything we know."

"Do you work with him often?" Yankton asked.

"As often as he lets us," Joe said, going on to answer other questions about Fenton Hardy's line of work as they made their way to the dining car. He was disappointed to find that the blond girls had vanished. He'd probably run into them again.

Frank spied Talia as soon as he entered the dining car. She was at a table near the middle, her camera lying in front of her. At the sight of him, she beamed and waved. He did likewise, walking toward her.

"Glad to see you could make it," Talia said, sliding over next to the window so Frank could sit beside her. She glanced at Yankton. "Who's this?"

"I'd like you to meet Sergeant Yankton of the Denver Police Department," Frank said. "Sergeant, this is Talia Neiman."

"Pleased to meet you," the officer said.

Talia stared silently at him for a moment. "I didn't know there were police on board," she said.

"Just me, and I'm helping Frank and Joe," Yankton explained, sitting down across from Frank.

Joe had taken the seat across from Talia and was sipping his water.

"Really?" Talia smiled at Frank. "You two

are just full of surprises." She was obviously puzzled by the officer's presence.

Frank shrugged sheepishly. "Our father arranged it."

"Is your father an officer?" Talia asked.

"He's a private investigator," Frank explained. He didn't want to launch into a long explanation, so he changed the subject instead. "Say, have you seen Curt Loring recently?"

Talia's forehead creased. "Loring? The man you introduced me to this morning? Is he still on the train?"

"Yes. We saw him a short while ago," Frank said.

"No, I haven't seen him," Talia said. "I just assumed he got off."

Joe was studying her camera, an expensive 35-mm model. "Mind if I look at this?" he asked, laying his hand on it.

Her gaze fixed on Frank, Talia shrugged and said, "Go right ahead."

"Thanks." Joe examined the camera carefully, noting that the shutter was set at a very high speed. He blinked in surprise. How could Talia have set it so high? That was all wrong for indoor photography, even with a flash. He adjusted the camera to a lower speed, listening to the clicks of each setting. Then he raised the camera and peered through the telephoto lens, scanning the car.

"Are you here because of the death of Andrew Driscoll?" Talia asked Sergeant Yankton.

Joe swept the camera back and forth, amazed at the magnification. People yards away appeared to be only inches from him.

"In part," Yankton said.

About to put down the camera, Joe suddenly spotted Felix Delray. The man was at the last table on the far end, wearing what appeared to be a new sports jacket. Probably bought to go with his new slacks.

"I heard that the police have a suspect in custody," Talia said.

Joe listened with half an ear. He saw Delray's lips moving, as if the man were talking to someone. But there was no one at his table.

"I can't discuss a case under investigation," Sergeant Yankton said. "Official policy."

"I understand," Talia said.

Leaning forward, Joe saw that Delray held a small, rectangular object in his left hand. He turned the lens, trying to get a clearer view. The object came into slightly sharper focus. It was a miniature tape recorder.

Delray raised his head and looked toward their table. The man's eyes narrowed. Then Delray glowered, stuck the recorder in his jacket pocket, and rose. Joe lowered the camera as the man came down the aisle toward them. He braced himself for an argument. To his surprise, Delray walked past without a glance and exited the car. Frank watched him go by, too.

"I'm glad that I'm only going to be on the train for a short while," Sergeant Yankton said. "I was given the assignment on such short notice, I didn't have time to bring a change of clothes or anything."

The statement made Joe's ears perk up. He realized that Delray must have boarded the train on short notice, too. Why else had the man worn the same clothes to Denver and then bought a new outfit? Someone on a business trip would never do such a thing. He looked at his brother, who apparently had the same thought.

"Will you excuse us for a bit," Frank addressed Talia and the officer, rising. "Joe and I have something to do.'

"Sure," Talia said.

"Give a yell if you need me," Yankton said.

Joe deposited the camera on the table and joined his brother in pursuit of Felix Delray.

Chapter

12

"ARE YOU THINKING what I'm thinking?" Joe said as they left the dining car.

"I think it's time for a showdown with Delray." Frank nodded grimly. "We've put it off long enough."

"Well, we've got something new to ask him about," Joe added. He told Frank about Delray's tape recorder. "And when he realized I was watching, he took off," he concluded.

"It sure seems as though he's up to something," Frank said, surveying the corridor for Delray.

As he stood there, he saw the conductor, Mr. Herman, chatting with an elderly woman.

Conductor Herman stepped into their path and held up his hand. "Hold on there, fellas. I'd like to talk to you."

"What's up?" Frank asked, smiling at the woman. She reminded him of his aunt Gertrude, back home in Bayport.

"Were either of you on the roof of the train a couple of minutes ago?" Herman asked.

Joe was taken aback. "What would we be doing up there?"

"With you two, there's no telling." The conductor nodded at the woman. "Mrs. Egan here was heading for the dining car. She'd just left her sleeper when she heard somebody walking over her head on the roof. Scared her half to death." He paused. "Given your track record, I thought it might have been one of you."

"It wasn't. We were with people in the dining car until a minute ago," Frank assured the man, turning to Mrs. Egan. "Would you tell us what happened?"

"There's not much to tell," she said. "I was on the platform between the second and third sleeping cars, heading for the dining car, when I heard someone walk over my head. The person just about gave me a heart attack."

"Sorry I accused you," Herman apologized, then blinked. "Goodness. This could mean we have *another* wild man aboard."

"I hope you find him," Frank said, and kept on going.

"My guess is that it was Curt Loring on the roof," Joe said.

"That would explain how we lost him earlier. He climbed onto the roof to get away from us. Then he jumped to the next car, where that woman heard him."

"It never occurred to me to check the roof," Frank said. He hadn't pictured Loring as the type to take such a risk. Only one thing could make the scientist pull such a stunt—Loring must be afraid for his life.

At Delray's compartment Frank knocked. No one answered. He took out his wallet and removed his plastic Bayport Library card. "Cover me," he said.

Joe stepped behind his brother, screening Frank from view. He glanced both ways. No one around. "Go for it," he said.

Sliding the wafer-thin card into the crack between the door and the jamb, Frank worked the hard plastic up and down. At the same time he jiggled the handle.

"Better hurry," Joe urged. A man was approaching, but he stuck his hands in his pockets and began whistling as if he didn't have a care in the world.

Frank frowned, afraid he was wasting his time. Come on! he wanted to shout. A second later there was a loud snap and the door swung in. "Come on," he said aloud, quickly stepping over the threshold.

After smiling pleasantly at the man, Joe entered. The light was on. He shut the door, leaned against it, and breathed a sigh of relief. "That was close."

"See what you can find," Frank said, moving to the closet. Hanging inside was the suit Delray had been wearing when they first met him, as rumpled as ever. "Just as I thought. He doesn't have any other clothes."

Joe pulled out the drawers in the small dresser. In one he found toothpaste and other toiletries, all brand-new. "It looks like he just stocked up on soap and stuff in Denver."

In the bottom of the closet Frank found the overnight bag. He unzipped it. "Empty." Turning, he saw a wastebasket in the corner. He walked over and saw a single slip of white paper at the bottom.

"Anything?" Joe asked.

Frank picked up the slip. "It's a receipt from a Denver store with today's date."

"But there's nothing to connect him to Andrew's death," Joe said. His gaze fell on a folded newspaper lying on an end table. He scooped it up, thinking it would be a Denver paper. Instead, it was the San Francisco *Chronicle*, open to the fourth page where an item had been circled in blue ink. He read the byline and said, "I think I've got a clue."

Hurrying over, Frank peered over his brother's shoulder. He was equally flabbergasted. The circled article was a science feature on viral research and the development of serums.

107

The story had been submitted by a reporter named Felix Delray.

A scratching sound came from the door as someone inserted a key in the lock. When the door opened, Delray stood there gaping at them in astonishment that swiftly changed to anger. "What do you think you're doing?" he demanded, striding toward Frank and slamming the door shut.

Frank wasn't about to be intimidated. He took the newspaper and shook it. "We should ask you the same thing. How did you find out about Professor Driscoll's research?"

Delray looked at the paper, then came forward to grab it from Frank's hand. "You had no business prying."

"You're a fine one to talk," Joe snapped. "You've been sticking your nose into our affairs since San Francisco."

"It's my job," Delray replied. "I'm a reporter."

"We know that now," Frank said. "But we thought you were working for the people who shot at us. Thanks to you, we wasted precious time."

Delray tossed the newspaper onto a chair. "I'm only trying to make a living. If Professor Driscoll had come clean from the start, I wouldn't even be here."

"What do you mean?" Joe asked.

"I heard through one of my sources that the

professor was working on something big for the government," Delray disclosed. "So I went to see him. He refused to confirm the story and wouldn't give me the time of day." He scowled. "I wasn't about to take that lying down, so I began spying on him, keeping track of his activities, trying to figure out what he was up to."

"You saw Andrew and us leave, and you trailed us," Frank deduced.

Delray nodded. "I hung far back so Andrew wouldn't spot me. When I saw the sniper attack, I knew I was onto something big. Naturally, I shadowed you to Oakland."

"Naturally," Joe echoed.

"I called in my general story about viral research, then bought a ticket to keep tabs on the three of you," Delray concluded.

"And since you didn't have any spare clothes, you had to buy a new outfit in Denver," Frank remarked.

"That, and the newspaper," Delray said. "So how about it? Will you tell me what's going on? Why was Andrew murdered? Who killed him?"

"Ask the police or scout it out," Frank said. He walked to the door. "You're the reporter, remember."

Joe was tempted to slam the door as he went out on his brother's heels, but didn't.

Frank headed down the passage and Joe followed. "Does this mean we're officially out of suspects?"

"Not if you count Loring," Frank said.

"Loring," Joe said. "Who has also gone into hiding."

"But who doesn't seem to be thinking straight if he's riding on top of the train," Frank added.

"So maybe we ought to find where he's hanging out." Joe grinned. "Or should that be hanging *on?*"

Frank frowned. "That Mrs. Egan was scared on her way from the sleeping cars to the dining room. So it would seem that Loring, if it was Loring, was moving toward the back of the train."

"I'll bet he's heading for the baggage car!" Joe exclaimed. "There's nobody there to hear any telltale footsteps from above."

Frank nodded. "Let's check it out."

The Hardys headed down the length of the train, until they reached the locked door of the baggage car. Joe paused. "How do we get up there?" he asked.

"We'll have to take a window out, and boost ourselves out through it and up. If Loring could do it, we can." After they removed the window, Frank laced his fingers together, making a cup out of his hands. "Put your toe in here, and I'll give you a boost. Then you can help me up."

With Frank's help, Joe made it onto the roof. From below, Frank heard Joe yell, "Hold it!" Then Joe's face appeared upside down in the window. "Loring's here, all right. But he's running for it! Come on!" Joe extended his arms.

Where can he go? Frank wondered as he climbed up. We've cut off Loring from the rest of the train. He can only make for the caboose.

That was exactly what Curt Loring was doing. By the time Frank reached the roof and the frigid nighttime air, the chemist had made his way halfway down the baggage car's eighty-foot length. Frank was grateful for the little light from the almost full moon and sky-ful of stars.

Joe, impetuous as ever, took off in full pursuit. He had to slow down when the wind caught him, though, and crawl on all fours.

Frank followed, but in a much slower crab-like posture. The train roof was curved, which made both boys' footing very uncertain. Also, because of the train's speed there seemed to be a gale force wind pushing against their backs. "Loring!" Frank finally yelled.

The chemist's only response was to put on a burst of speed.

Frank was far behind when Loring reached the end of the car. The scientist didn't slow down, though. He pushed himself to crawl a little faster, then hurled himself over the accordion-ridged divider between the baggage car and caboose. He landed on top of the caboose and continued on.

Joe reached the accordion gap between the baggage car and caboose and hurled himself over. Now he was only a few yards behind Loring.

Then it was Frank's turn. He forced all the power he could from his legs and leapt. He tried not to think about how far he'd fall if he missed and slid off the side to be dragged or crushed to his death.

He hit the caboose roof, staggered, then steadied himself. Ahead of him, Loring had reached the end of the line and was standing stiffly upright at the far edge of the caboose roof, staring down at the tracks below.

Joe approached him and clapped a hand on Loring's shoulder.

At the touch, Loring suddenly broke out of his trance. He swung an arm back and caught Joe in the chest.

The unexpected blow knocked Joe off balance. He tottered back, his arms windmilling wildly as he fought for his balance on the curved roof.

"Joe!" Frank yelled, running for his brother. But Joe fell, tumbling toward the side of the roof—

And then he went over!

Chapter

13

FRANK FELL FLAT to his stomach, almost slipping off the roof as he reached for Joe. He was a second too late. His brother was gone!

"Oh, Joe!" he gasped.

"Frank!" a voice came from below him. Disbelieving, Frank peered over the edge. Joe's blond hair shone in the moonlight several feet down. He was clinging to the rungs of a ladder welded to the side of the caboose.

"Are you okay?" Frank called anxiously, his words almost carried away by the roar of the wind.

"I feel like I just got hit by a football team's offensive line," Joe yelled back. "But I'll make it up in a minute. Where's Loring?" he asked very slowly so Frank would hear.

Frank glanced at Loring. He hadn't taken the opportunity to double back toward the front of the train. Instead, he was now clambering over the edge, apparently heading for the rear door of the caboose.

"He's trying to get into the caboose!" Frank yelled.

"Well? Go get him!"

Loring was gone by the time Frank reached the end of the roof. Peering over, Frank saw how he must have used a pair of stanchions welded to the back of the door frame as footholds and then handholds to get inside.

Taking a deep breath of icy air, Frank swung over. He rested a foot on top of a handlelike steel bar, then reached for the one on the other side with his foot. Then he moved his hands down beside his feet and kicked his feet free. The door was open, so he could swing his body inside.

The dark room in front of him wasn't empty, though. Curt Loring was there!

With a wild cry, the chemist kicked out at Frank, his foot catching Frank in the stomach. One of his hands was torn free from its stanchion!

Frank swung back dizzily, his arm feeling as if it would be ripped from the socket as he tried to cling to his lone handhold.

Loring was yelling like a crazy man, lashing

out with his foot. Each blow that connected sent Frank a little closer to doom.

"Frank!" Joe's horrified voice blared from above. He stared down from the roof of the caboose, helpless to save his brother.

"What's going on here?" an angry voice demanded from deep within the caboose.

Loring glanced over his shoulder, and Frank pulled himself together for a last desperate move. Pivoting on his single handhold, he swung himself into the car and dropped to the floor. Loring had his back to Frank, and that was all the advantage Frank needed. He pounced on the man, ignoring the pain in his arm, and brought him down.

Then he saw who had distracted Loring—it was Herman, the train conductor. The man had slipped off his uniform jacket and cap, his tie undone and his collar button open.

"Frank Hardy!" he exclaimed. "I can't even catch a little shut-eye without you—"

His eyes suddenly flicked to the door. "Oh, and Joe Hardy, too! Now the cast is complete!"

Herman stared down at Loring, who had gone completely limp as soon as Frank tackled him. "And who is this guy?"

"This is your rooftop flyer, Mr. Herman," Frank said. "His name is Curt Loring, and we have a lot of questions for him."

"Loring, Loring," the conductor seemed to be running through a passenger list in his mind. "Right! Why don't you take him to his compartment, and tell him to stay put."

They marched the now-docile Loring through the caboose and up to the baggage car, where the conductor unlocked the doors. Then they continued the length of the train to the chemist's roomette.

Loring walked in silence and gave up his room key wordlessly.

Frank stepped in, flipping on the light. The room was still a shambles. Obviously, Loring had never returned earlier.

Joe led Loring to the seat, letting the door swing closed behind him. "Sit," he said, "and start talking."

Loring collapsed onto the seat, his head in his hands. "I thought you were them." His voice was shaky. "When I saw someone climbing onto the roof, I didn't even look at your faces. I just figured you had to be them."

He peered up at Frank from between his fingers. "When you came after me, I was so scared that I didn't recognize you until after you tackled me. Before that, I tried—I—I—" He clenched his hands tightly in his lap. "I nearly *killed* you. If the conductor hadn't come along—I'm sorry. I thought you were one of them, coming to get me. They'll get me sooner or later, anyway."

"Who's 'them'?" Joe wanted to know.

"The ones after the vials." Loring gazed

fearfully up at them. "Help me—protect me, and I'll help you and tell you everything you want to know." He gulped as if he were about to cry. "I don't want to die."

"We can't do much protecting till we know what we're up against," Joe said grimly. "Start talking."

Loring sighed. "It all started about four months ago. A man who called himself Steiner was waiting in my apartment one day after work. He offered me a lot of money to keep him informed about the professor's work on the new serum."

"How did Steiner know about the project?" Frank asked.

"He told me his organization had contacts in high places," Loring said with a shrug.

"What organization?" Joe pressed.

"I don't think they have a name. Steiner wouldn't tell me much about them. I got the impression they're big, and into a lot of heavy business—extortion, industrial espionage, dirty tricks—that kind of stuff," Loring said. "Once he mentioned that they've been in business for years."

"What did you do?" Frank asked.

"I should have told Steiner to get lost." Loring drew in a long breath. "But he offered me a hundred thousand dollars—in cash. Do you know what a research chemist makes these days? Especially someone who has to play third fiddle on a research team? And all I had to do was pass along a little information.''

Frank remembered the slip of paper he'd found—the one with the phone number with the San Francisco area code. Starland must be in the 408 area code, so it would be long distance to call San Francisco from there. "So you called Steiner in San Francisco to report.''

Loring gaped at him. "How did you know?''

"Just keep talking,'' Joe cut in.

"Everything went without a hitch until the professor completed the serum. Then Steiner wanted to know where it was kept at night. I told him about the lab where Professor Driscoll did most of his work.''

"You must have realized by then that Steiner would try to steal the serum,'' Joe said.

The chemist slowly nodded. "But by then I was in too deep. There was nothing I could do.'' He ran a hand across his forehead. "If the serum had been where it was supposed to be when they broke in, this nightmare would be over.''

"But it wasn't, was it?'' Joe said. "Professor Driscoll moved it to another department.''

"Right.'' Loring shuddered. "Then Steiner started getting scary. He told me that either I made certain he got those vials, or I'd end up as fish food in the Pacific Ocean.''

Frank watched Loring shiver at the memory. "Do you think Steiner is the head man of this ring of crooks?" he asked.

"At first I thought he was," Loring admitted. "But Steiner let it slip once that he reported to someone higher up."

"I guess you're the one who let it leak that Professor Driscoll had called our father," Joe said. "We could see how happy you were to see us."

"That's right. Steiner decided to slow you down, then grab the professor to get the vials."

"It might have been a good plan—until we interfered," Joe said.

Loring's face became pinched. "That's when things got really bad. Steiner called me from a pay phone right after you guys left the facility. I told him about your plan. He ordered me to find out which security firm was going to transport the vials."

"And did you?" Frank asked.

"I went upstairs and listened at the professor's door again." Loring shook his head. "The first call he made was to a local kennel to board his dog. He called the security firm next. When he hung up, he started laughing. I could hear him puttering around in his office, saying, 'Now, what can I give to those guys that will look like the real thing?' I hid just as he went out to go to the lab."

119

"Where was our father while all this was going on?" Joe wanted to know.

"Out front, waiting for the professor." Loring ducked his head. "Your father never saw me."

Frank had almost all the pieces of the mystery together now. "So you told Steiner about what the professor did?"

Loring nodded. "He'd given me the number of the pay phone and told me to call back."

"So Steiner figured either the professor had the vials, or we did. He probably had us covered all the way—right up to someone available to act as a sniper."

"How did the guy at the house know to shoot at us?" Joe asked.

Frank shrugged. "A code word over a mobile phone could have set that up." He frowned at Loring. "There's only one thing I don't understand."

"What's that?" Loring asked.

"Why didn't Steiner save himself a lot of trouble by just having you steal the vials?"

Loring shook his head. "Easier said than done. The professor and Andrew never left me, or anybody else, alone with their precious serum. And only the professor and Andrew knew the combination to the professor's safe."

"Did Steiner order you to get on this train?" Joe asked.

Licking his lips nervously, Loring nodded.

"I was supposed to find out if Andrew had the vials. But before I could, Andrew turned up dead. Then *my* compartment was ransacked. I realized that Steiner must think I was holding out on him, or worse, that I'd gotten hold of the vials myself and was keeping them."

Joe leaned against the wall. "So you started running."

"I always thought Steiner was dangerous." Loring's face was dead white. "But after he killed Andrew I knew I was in deep trouble. First I tried hiding in empty compartments, and finally wound up on top of the train."

"Why did you run the time we saw you?" Frank asked.

"I was going to ask for your help, but I saw this man following you and figured he must be one of Steiner's people." Loring was trembling again. "It's only a matter of time before he gets me."

Frank was amazed! Loring had been hiding so long, he didn't know about the tall man's arrest. "Steiner's not going anywhere for a while," Frank said. "The police have him, back in Denver."

Loring's jaw fell open. "They got him? I had no idea. I hid in an empty compartment for the whole Denver layover." For the first time the man on the couch seemed to relax.

"Why didn't you get off the train in Denver and run for it?" Joe asked.

"I figured Steiner would have people watching the train," Loring admitted. "I was afraid to take the chance."

"Well, I'd say you have only one chance now," Joe said. "There's a Denver cop aboard the train. He's probably still in the dining car. If you turned yourself in to him—"

"I don't—noooooooo!" Loring suddenly stared at the door, screamed in terror, and leaped to his feet.

Joe whipped around and saw that the door was ajar. In the opening he could see a gun barrel with a silencer. Frank and Loring were both on their feet with no place to hide. In the cramped room, killing them would be like shooting fish in a barrel.

Yelling at the top of his lungs, Joe shoved his brother and Loring in opposite directions as a flash leapt from the gun muzzle.

Chapter

14

THE PISTOL was fired twice, the silenced shots sounding like angry coughs. Joe dove for the door, hoping that Frank and Curt Loring had fallen out of the line of fire.

One bullet passed close enough for him to feel the air stir. Behind him, he heard a scream. It was Loring.

Joe charged the door, but didn't catch the mystery gunman's weapon or wrist. They were yanked outside, out of sight, before the door slammed closed. Staying low, in case their attacker decided to shoot through the door panel, Joe turned to see what had happened in the room.

Curt Loring lay sprawled across the seat,

his face pale, a wound oozing at the side of his head. The man's eyes were closed, and his breathing came in ragged gasps.

Frank knelt over him, examining the injury. "I think the bullet just creased him," he whispered, "but we need a doctor here."

The brothers exchanged glances. Stepping into the corridor outside could be deadly if the gunman was still around. They wouldn't know that until the door was opened, though.

Joe took a deep breath and slowly eased the door open. A quick peek showed him that the corridor was empty. The shooter must have fled.

"Anything?" Frank asked in a low voice.

Joe stuck his head back in. "No. I'm going to get Sergeant Yankton and the conductor."

"And a doctor."

"I'm on my way. Lock the door." Joe raced down the corridor.

Frank sorted through the mess in the compartment, gathering enough clean material to make a pressure pad to slow the bleeding. Andrew, Loring—who else would be hurt, or worse, killed, before this was over?

Frank could barely control the anger he felt toward Loring. The man had taken money to betray the Driscolls, then got caught up in his own greed. What a case! An assistant who's working for the other side, a client who thinks that boarding the family dog is more important than following plans.

Frank straightened. Wait a second. What was that pamphlet they'd found in Andrew's compartment? The one about caring for your dog? The title came back in a rush. "Seven Things Every New Dog Owner Should Know."

New dog owners? Had the Driscolls gotten their pet recently?

Curt Loring's eyes fluttered open. "Hurt," he whined. "Feel—awful."

His eyes started to shut, but Frank leaned over him. "Curt," he said, "can you answer a question?"

Loring opened his eyes again, but his expression was vague. He was dreadfully pale. Frank kept up the pressure with the pad, making Loring wince. "Ow."

"You said Professor Driscoll boarded his dog at a kennel," Frank said. "How long have the Driscolls had the dog?"

For a second Loring stared at him. "Don't know. Ten years? It's an old mutt." He closed his eyes and groaned.

Ten years? A crazy idea formed in Frank's mind. But he couldn't check it out until Joe got back. Long minutes passed before he heard running footsteps in the passage outside.

"Open up!" Joe called, knocking. Frank opened the door.

"We were lucky. I found the sergeant and I got an attendant to find the conductor."

Sergeant Yankton stood in the doorway. "Let's take a look," he said, coming in. Frank moved the pressure pad, and the sergeant nodded. "He's lucky it just creased the side of his head. You've just about got the bleeding stopped." They replaced the pad. "Tell me how it happened."

Frank quickly ran through their interrogation and the attack. As he finished, more footsteps sounded outside, and Conductor Herman ran in.

"This trip is turning into a nightmare," he muttered. "In here, Doctor."

A man carrying a black medical bag hastened in and knelt beside Loring. "I'm Dr. Benjamin," he said.

The conductor glanced at Frank and Joe. "Could I speak to you two outside while the doctor examines his patient?"

"Sure." Joe led the way into the corridor, Frank following. The conductor shut the door. "I'd just gotten a message from the engineer when the attendant found me," Herman said. "We've received an emergency call from the Omaha dispatcher about your father."

Joe leaned closer. "What about him?"

"Fenton Hardy and Professor Driscoll are flying by private jet from Chicago to Omaha,"

Sherman said. "From there, they're taking a helicopter to meet us along the way."

"We could use some reinforcements," Frank admitted.

"I'd better get back inside to find out what the doctor has to say." Herman went back inside.

"Too bad about Loring," Joe said. "Now we've got nothing left."

"Maybe not," Frank said. "Remember that pamphlet we found? The one about being a new dog owner? Well, the Driscolls have had a mutt for ten years."

Joe's eyes widened. "I never bothered to mention it, but I found dog treats in Andrew's pocket."

Frank started excitedly for the end of the train. "Do you think he could have smuggled a dog on the baggage car?"

"I think he could have," Joe said, tearing after his brother. "I just thought of something else. When Andrew brought me that hamburger from the dining car, he mentioned that he'd stopped off on his way back to get it. That means he was coming from someplace *beyond* the dining car. The baggage car?"

Frank felt surer and surer about the answer to his question. If he turned out to be right, they'd have the vials in their hands very soon. As they passed through the dining car, he looked around for Talia. "Hey, Joe, did you see Talia when you went for Yankton?"

"Nope," Joe said.

"No big deal." Frank figured she'd be waiting in her compartment. After all, they *had* disappeared for a long time.

At last they reached the baggage car. After removing a lock pick tool from his back pocket, Frank went to work on the door. Three or four minutes later the heavy door eased open, and Frank and Joe exchanged excited glances. Was their long hunt finally coming to an end? Turning on the overhead lights, the boys systematically searched the long car, listening for any animal shufflings or barks. If Andrew had smuggled a pet on board, it would have to be wildly hungry and scared. Both boys hoped Andrew had left enough water for the animal.

Joe heard it first—it almost sounded like an infant crying. Tiny puppy whimperings came from just a few feet away.

Frank pulled two trunks to one side and behind them found a plastic kennel with a cute Boston terrier puppy. It started dancing excitedly. Its rear end was swishing back and forth so fast, it knocked over a full dish of water.

Joe noticed a sticker on the side of the cage. He moved closer and saw that it was a price tag from a store in Oakland called Animal

World. "The address is on the same street as the train station."

Frank bent over the cage, which seemed far too large for such a small dog. He noticed that the rear had been blocked off with cardboard. Opening the cage, he scooped up the puppy. "Would you mind holding him for a second?" he asked Joe.

"Can you guarantee he won't leak?" Joe asked.

Reaching inside, Frank pulled out the make-shift barrier.

"Well?" Joe said. "Are they in there?"

A second later Frank drew out a small box that had been hidden in the rear. He clicked it open. Resting in a padded lining inside were two laboratory vials.

"Is that what I think it is?" Joe asked as he returned the puppy to the cage.

"It sure is," Frank began. Then he heard a distinctive *click* from behind them. He swung around, hiding the vials behind him.

But it was Talia, only six feet away, grinning as she put her camera down. A brown bag hung from her shoulder. "Where did you come from?" Frank asked.

"I was looking for you when I saw the two of you heading for the rear of the train." Talia moved closer. "I followed to see what was going on. You made a great picture with that cage."

Joe glanced up at the dim overhead lighting. "Shouldn't you have used a flash?"

Talia laughed. "I suppose I should have thought of that." She reached into her bag. "Luckily, I've got one here."

Joe frowned. How could a professional photojournalist forget something as basic as a flash?

"Now just get back around the cage," Talia said.

In the next instant her hand came out of the bag—with a gun.

Before Frank or Joe could move, she had them both covered.

"Just hold that pose," Talia said, grinning.

Frank froze, stunned.

"Now take that little box from behind your back and put it on that trunk," Talia directed. "No tricks. You should know that I can use this gun."

He had no choice. Frank did as she directed, staring at the gun. It was a small-caliber automatic with a silencer. "I know you can. You just used it on Loring."

"He started making trouble for me," Talia said matter-of-factly. "Just as Andrew Driscoll did, waking up while I was searching his room. I hadn't planned to kill him. Only choke him unconscious, then question him. But he struggled, and things went a little too far. I thought you were Driscoll yesterday, Joe, when you walked into his compartment."

Frank and Joe glanced at each other. That was why she'd tried to strangle Joe. From the very beginning, Talia had been playing them like prize chumps.

"Oh, don't look so sad, Frank," she said. "I did like you. It's just that I thought you'd be useful as well. And you were. You did eventually lead me to the vials."

"So you're Steiner's boss," Frank said. "Were you running things all along?"

Talia smiled. "You've got it wrong, Frank. You ask questions when you've *got* a gun, not when you're facing one."

"Humor me," Frank said.

She laughed out loud. "All right. I'll tell you for the sake of a past friendship. I *am* Steiner's superior. But he was in charge of this operation. I stepped in only when he botched the daylight attempt on the lab."

"So you started off with the sniper attack on the van," Joe said.

"That was me, dear." Talia laughed. "When Steiner told me about your little shell game strategy, I moved to cover the Driscoll house, figuring they might stop there to pack. When the van arrived, I decided to try a quick fix and ambush you."

"But it didn't work," Joe said. "Because that lady drove up."

"I did hear where you were going, though. So I turned up at the station, ready to meet you. With Steiner and Loring on board also, I thought I had the situation covered. But as you know, some things went wrong—until now. Enough questions and answers," Talia said briskly. "Turn around, boys."

Joe's muscles tensed. The gun muzzle flicked up to cover his head.

"Try anything and you'll get worse than Loring did." Talia's voice was like steel. Frustrated, the boys turned around.

"Good. I'd like us to part on friendly terms," Talia said. "After all, you've done me a favor. This antidote will make me millions."

"Planning to sell it to the highest bidder?" Frank asked.

"Oh, no, I've got a buyer lined up already—a chemical company that desperately needs a new product." She chuckled. "None of the other industrial and government secrets I've stolen can compare with the profit on this operation."

"What about Steiner?" Frank stalled. "He's bound to confess to the police."

"He won't talk," Talia said confidently. "He knows what happens to people who do."

"Which leads into what happens to us?" Frank asked.

"I don't want to spoil the surprise," Talia said. "There's a coil of rope on top of that crate to your left, Frank. Why not use it to tie your brother up?''

Silently, Frank complied. Talia watched from over his shoulder. "Oh, you can do better than that. Make the knots *tight*. And you, Joe, don't try that old tensing-the-muscles trick." Her voice went cold again. "Unless you want to be dead, rather than tied."

When Frank finished, she complimented him on the job. "And don't feel bad about losing. I really enjoyed our little friendship, if it's any consolation."

"It's not," Frank said.

"Too bad." Talia stood behind him now. The hand with the gun quickly flew up and then swept down right onto Frank's head. Frank toppled to the floor. Joe thrashed around, trying to break the ropes. He couldn't.

"Such excitement over a little bop on the head," Talia said.

"You'll be caught," Joe said.

"Will I?" Talia opened the little carrying case to look at the vials inside. She read the labels aloud. "Mutated virus sample. You know what this is?"

"No."

"You're a poor liar, Joe Hardy. I know how Professor Driscoll developed a deadlier virus strain. I could probably sell this as a biological weapon, but I think I'll use it as a distraction.

It's easy to escape if the local law has something else to think about. And this little vial could keep them very busy."

She held the virus up to the light. "Soon death will flow through this train. The passengers don't know it, but the only way they're getting off this train will be in coffins."

Chapter

15

JOE COULD ONLY WATCH helplessly as Talia tied up his brother. She searched the shelves and came up with a dusty cloth. Tearing it into two strips, she slipped a gag around Frank's mouth. Then it was Joe's turn.

"Open wide," she said, tapping his chin with the silencer.

Joe had no choice. In a moment he was choking on rough, dusty fabric.

"Thank you," Talia said sweetly.

Joe remained still, but as soon as Talia took the vial carrier and left the car, he surged against his bonds. It was hopeless. His wrists and ankles were tied, then connected with a short length of rope. He could hardly move!

Twisting around, Joe nudged Frank's body

with his shoulder. Did Talia mean that she was going to kill everyone on board with the virus? Was that the kind of deadly distraction she had in mind?

Time crawled as Joe struggled against his ropes. He was ready to give up when he heard his brother groan.

Frank's eyes fluttered open, then went wide. He tried to speak, and ended up sputtering into the gag. Then Frank's eyes opened even wider, and he stared at an empty glass bottle in the corner. Joe understood. They needed a tool to get out of this! Grunting, he inched toward the bottle on his side.

Frank surged to his knees, tottering for a second, afraid the pain from his wrists and ankles would make him black out. Joe finally reached the bottle, nudging it with his nose to knock it over. Then he shoved it with his chin, sending it rolling to his brother.

Now it was Frank's turn. He made a clumsy backward catch, lifted the bottle, and smacked it against the floor. It didn't break.

Holding the bottle by its neck, he set off for a nearby metal trunk. He gave the bottle a clumsy swing, and was rewarded with the sound of smashing glass.

Carefully, Frank found a jagged section and he and Joe worked their way together. Back to back, Frank set to work sawing Joe's ropes.

136

The glass was slippery in Frank's sweat-slick hand, and with the ropes on his wrists cutting off his circulation, his fingers were almost numb. He was afraid he'd cut Joe—or himself. But strand by strand, Joe's ropes did fray and part.

With one giant wrench, Joe snapped the rope on his wrists. After yanking the gag from his mouth, he took the glass from Frank and set to work on his ankles.

Free at last, Joe turned to Frank. "We've got to stop Talia," he said, removing Frank's gag. "She threatened to kill everyone on the train to ensure her escape."

"How could I have even liked her?" Frank said, disgusted with himself.

"Hey." Joe grinned as he cut the ropes at Frank's wrists. "In her weird way, I think she liked you. I mean, shooting us would have been a lot less work."

"I just hope I can make Talia regret it," Frank said, tearing the ropes free.

He started down the aisle. "We have to report this to the conductor and Yankton. On the way we'll check Talia's compartment."

"I'm right behind you," Joe assured him.

The door to Talia's roomette was unlocked. Frank went in first. Talia wasn't there, although her clothes were still hanging in the closet. "She could be anywhere by now," he said grimly.

They headed for Loring's compartment. Sergeant Yankton and the conductor were just coming out the door.

"Good news," Yankton told them. "The doctor thinks Loring will come through okay."

"He may not," Frank said. "We found out who killed Andrew and shot Loring. But she now has the means to kill everyone who is peacefully asleep aboard this train."

The officer and conductor both stared in shock.

Frank gave them a quick explanation about the vials and about Talia Neiman's criminal organization. "She apparently intends to use the virus to cover her escape," he finished.

"All we can do is start looking for her," Yankton said. "I hope you never withhold information from the police again—it's not fair to keep us uninformed."

They split into teams, Joe and the sergeant, Frank and the conductor, and began working from each end of the train. Armed with passkeys, they invaded every compartment, even if their knocks went unanswered.

After searching two cars, Joe began to have doubts. Talia wouldn't let herself be caught so easily. As Loring had proved, there were too many hiding places on the train.

Frank refused to give up hope even after three hours. With all the sleeping cars thoroughly searched, he wanted to go on.

The four were now sitting in the dining car, drinking cups of instant coffee to stay awake. Suddenly Herman pointed out the window. "Hey, look, there's your helicopter."

Joe pressed his face tight against the window so he wouldn't see himself reflected in the nighttime glass. He raised his eyes skyward. A copter was keeping pace with the train. "It's got to be Dad and the professor."

As Frank joined him to stare out the window, the train began to brake. They appeared to be in a desolate area, with no houses or businesses in sight. Flat prairie land stretched out on one side of the train. On the other was a narrow field, bounded by what looked like a ravine. It was hard to see in the dark.

"What's going on?" the boys could hear sleepy people asking as they made their way into the dining car. All the windows were now crowded with curious passengers in robes and pajamas. They got quite a show, as the copter swooped down out of the starry sky to land beside the train.

"Come on," Frank said, heading for the exit with Joe right behind. They jumped to the ground and were startled by how cold it was. They waved to the figures emerging from the helicopter that had put down in the narrow field. "Dad! Professor!"

Joe had never seen his father so grave, and

Professor Driscoll's face was a mask of grief as they walked over to the boys.

"Have you found the vials?" the professor asked, his words accented by tiny puffs of warm white air.

"Found them and lost them," Frank had to admit. "A woman named Talia Neiman has them now."

The professor staggered back, his face a deathly pallor.

"Not only that," Joe said, picking up the story, "she's threatening to use the virus to kill people on the train to cover her escape."

"She could easily do that," the professor said. "The new virus works on the respiratory system in minutes. Contamination is horribly easy. You could inhale it, ingest it—even getting a trace on your skin could prove fatal."

"Maybe you should evacuate the train," Frank suggested to the conductor.

"If that's our only option—" Herman said. "I guess half the train is gathered together already."

Frank studied all the curious faces inside lining the windows and outside lining the track. Then he noticed something strange.

Up by the engines, a rather thin attendant had emerged and was now heading for the helicopter. The man's cap was pulled down low on his head, and his arms were crossed, pulling his uniform jacket tight across his body.

140

What's that guy doing? Frank wondered. Carrying something? Straining his eyes, he saw a small black box in the man's hands, and realized the awful truth. "It's her!" he shouted, sprinting for the chopper.

Talia had almost reached the helicopter when Frank raised the alarm. She ran the last few steps, whipping out her pistol as she leapt into the cockpit. The gun butt clipped the copter pilot in the side of the head. She tossed him out, her blond hair falling down as the cap fell off.

Then the copter rotors began to spin.

Frank was the closest to the chopper and he took off, his arms and legs pumping wildly. He had to stop Talia before she got away!

He still had yards to go as the helicopter began to rise.

Frank did the only thing he could. Adding a final burst of speed, he took three steps, then jumped!

The bottom skid of the helicopter was just above his head. He reached out and grabbed hold.

At the same moment the chopper swept into the sky, carrying him upward at a crazy angle, dangling over the gorge.

Chapter
16

FRANK CLUNG HELPLESSLY from the skid on the passenger side of the helicopter. He could no longer see to the bottom of the rocky gorge, but remembered jagged boulders at its bottom. If I slip, he thought, I won't have a happy landing.

Still worse, the chopper seemed to be bucking and jumping, lurching drunkenly across the dark sky. The wild movement almost made Frank lose his grip as the runner he clung to dipped more than a foot. My extra weight must be giving Talia piloting problems, he realized. The aircraft hovered as she tried to regain control.

Frank could see Joe, his father, Yankton, and Herman down on the ground, running toward the gorge. They had to be shouting, but Frank couldn't hear a thing over the roar of the helicopter engine and rotors. He knew he had to get inside the chopper while it was stabilizing.

Swinging his legs out and twisting in midair, Frank managed to throw a knee over the skid he was clinging to. He pushed up, reaching for the handle to the door.

His fingers were just inches short when the helicopter bucked again, climbing straight up. Frank was nearly thrown off. He lunged for the door handle, caught hold, and tore it open.

Talia was desperately working the control sticks, but she stared at Frank in amazement. Then she let one stick go to grab for the pistol that lay on the control console beside her.

Half in the door, Frank saw the muzzle of the silencer pointed straight at him. There was no way he could duck out of the line of fire.

But without Talia's hand on the stick, the helicopter banked sharply, going into a steep dive. Her arm was thrown upward.

Frank used the momentum of the dive to leap into the cockpit, scraping his shins on the door frame. The helicopter seemed to tumble in the air. He dove across the console and grabbed her wrist.

"I'll shoot!" Talia yelled over the engine noise.

Frank twisted her wrist, forcing her to

143

release the pistol. He glanced out the cockpit to see the moonlit boulders of the gorge sweeping up to meet them. "Pull out or we're history," he yelled.

Talia's eyes were round. She grabbed the control sticks, fighting to bring the helicopter out of its dive.

For five terrifying seconds, Frank thought she couldn't do it. He slid into the passenger seat, scooping up the pistol as he watched the shadowy boulders grow larger and larger in the soft moonlight. The aircraft was less than fifty feet above them when suddenly it tilted upward again and streaked over the terrain.

Frank pointed the pistol at Talia. "Land in the field near Joe and the others," he said.

Talia glanced at the small box wedged between the console and her seat. "Let me get away with the serum and I'll give you half of what I make on it."

"Don't waste your breath," Frank told her.

Shoulders sagging, Talia reduced speed and brought the helicopter around.

On the ground, Joe saw the change in course and whooped, "All right! He did it!" He rushed forward as the helicopter landed, bending over to avoid the spinning rotors.

Opening the passenger door, he found Frank inside, covering Talia with her own pistol. "Here," his brother said, handing over the vial carrier.

Joe carefully took the small box as his father and the other men closed in. He saw Sergeant Yankton go around, take Talia from the cockpit, and slip handcuffs on her wrists. It's over, he told himself. She's caught.

Frank stepped down a little dizzily. Fenton clapped his son on the back. "Well done."

"Thank you, young man," Professor Driscoll said. "At least I won't go down in history as a mass murderer."

From behind them came a spiteful laugh. "Don't be so sure of that, Professor."

Joe turned to see Sergeant Yankton leading Talia over to them. Even in handcuffs, she grinned confidently.

"What are you talking about?" the professor demanded angrily.

"Take a look in that little box," Talia told him. "I think you'll understand."

Afraid of what he'd find, Joe opened the box. Even in the dark he could tell there was only one vial in the box—the one marked Serum.

"Guess where the virus is?" Talia said, nodding toward the train. "I've rigged it with a little charge. It's set to go off in five or six minutes. Everyone on board will be exposed to your pet bug, Driscoll. You'll have a death train on your hands."

Professor Driscoll recoiled, horrified. "You wouldn't!"

"I have nothing to lose," Talia told him, waggling her handcuffs. "There's only one way to save those lives. Release me, and once I'm airborne, I'll tell you where the bomb is."

Joe snapped the lid closed. "No way," he rapped out. "You're not walking away from this."

Talia shrugged. "Suit yourself. But you'll never find the bomb in time. The deaths of everyone on board will be on your hands."

Conductor Herman stared at his train in horror. "What can we do? She's got us over a barrel."

Frank frowned. There was no way they could clear the whole train in minutes. And as they knew, it would take hours to search for the bomb. "If only we had some clue," he muttered.

Joe straightened up. "We do," he said. "Back in the baggage car, she said that death would *flow* through the train. Now, she doesn't seem the poetic type."

Frank noticed how Talia was glaring at his brother. The word *flow* must mean something, but what. "Water!" he burst out. "The bomb must be in the water supply!"

The conductor leaned forward. "There's a boiler room in the car behind the engines," he said. "It supplies water for the whole train."

"That must be it!" Frank yelled running for the train. "Come on, Joe!"

146

Joe gave the remaining vial to the professor and followed at top speed.

"Be careful," Fenton called after them. "We'll start evacuating the train just in case."

As he ran to the car, Frank saw countless faces staring out the windows of the train. The lives of all those people depend on us, he thought, putting on more speed.

Joe saw the two high school girls, Sally and Ruth, pointing and waving to them. Sorry, he thought. I don't have time for you now. They had reached the right car and were mounting the steps.

Just inside was a narrow hall. Frank followed it, to find the way blocked by a door with the sign Boiler Room: Authorized Personnel Only. "This is it," he said, reaching for the handle. The door was locked.

"No time for keys. Kick it open," Joe said.

Frank launched a karate kick at the lock. The door trembled, but held.

"We'll do it together," Joe said, moving beside his brother. "On the count of two. Ready? One—"

"Two!" Together, their heels smashed above and below the lock. Metal snapped, and the door swung open.

Joe whistled at the sight of the enormous boiler and the network of pipes leading from it. "That sucker must hold hundreds of gallons," he said.

Frank was already scanning the system. No bomb on any of the pipes he could see. Where would Talia have put it?

Joe circled the other side, glancing at his watch. "We've got three minutes, tops," he announced.

"Thanks for the reminder." Frank stared at the top of the boiler, a foot above his head. Up there would be the logical place, he figured.

Joe found a stepladder propped against one wall. He grabbed it and leaned it against the side of the boiler. "Up you go."

Frank was still below the rim of the boiler when he heard the faint ticking. He reached the top of the ladder and saw the bomb, located dead center atop the water tank. "Got it!" he said.

"Can you dismantle it?" Joe asked.

Frank examined the bomb. It was a flat pancake of plastic explosive, with the vial buried in the middle and a timer set on top. He scraped the whole thing off the metal and brought it close.

"Two minutes left," Joe said.

Frank had the bomb in his hands now. There were four wires running from the timer. Disarming the bomb would take too long. He carefully climbed down the ladder.

"We'll have to get this outside, away from the train," Frank said. As they reached the car exit, he dug into the pliable mass of explosive, working the vial free. Joe was already outside, staring up at him.

Frank finally extracted the vial. "I've got the virus," he said.

"And we've got ninety seconds," Joe reported. "Give me the bomb. I'll get it out of here."

He reached up, snatching the deadly packet from Frank's hand. "I'll try to reach the gorge," he said, already running.

If I can get this thing down there, Joe thought, the gorge walls should protect the train from any blast.

He ran with the bomb held close to his chest, like a pass receiver running for a field goal. But no football had ever ticked its way to doom as he carried it.

"He's got it!" Sergeant Yankton yelled.

Paying no attention, Joe ran for the gorge. The ground wasn't level and it was dark, so he couldn't go all-out for fear of falling. The thought of stumbling in a rut or prairie dog hole sent cold sweat running down his back in the freezing weather.

The lip of the gorge was right ahead, now. Did he have five seconds left? Three? One?

Whipping his arm back like a discus thrower, he sent the pancake-bomb sailing into the middle of the gorge. The most dangerous Frisbee I know, he thought.

The bomb arced down among the boulders, and Joe threw himself backward, not a heartbeat too soon.

A tremendous blast shook the air, sending up a small mushroom cloud of shattered stone. Joe lay flat on his back as debris spattered down all around him. The danger was past. He'd done it.

Ten minutes later Frank and Joe stood near the dining car, shivering as they watched Sergeant Yankton escort Talia Neiman into the helicopter. Curt Loring was already on board, as was Professor Driscoll with his precious vials.

Talia had the nerve to raise her cuffed hands in a wave. Frank did not respond. "I hope we never bump into her again," he said.

"Oh, I don't think that's too likely." Joe gave him a grin. "She's going to be behind bars for a long time."

"I'd almost guarantee that," Fenton Hardy said, coming up. He grinned proudly. "You did well, boys."

"Thanks, Dad." Frank had a hard time accepting the praise, though. They should have done better, suspecting Talia, protecting Andrew—no, this was not a perfect case. "How is Loring?" he asked.

"The doctor said he's okay, but wants him in a hospital. We'll drop him off in North

Platte." He looked at the almost-full copter. "Sorry I can't offer you a lift. But a nice, quiet train ride is just what you need to unwind." He headed for the helicopter.

"See you in Chicago," Joe called after him.

As Fenton climbed into the chopper, Frank could see Talia in the lit up cockpit. She gazed over at him, smiling mysteriously. Then the copter slowly started to rise.

"So that's it," Joe said with a sigh. "The professor is taking the antidote to Chicago, Talia is out of business, and I'm starving. Let's see if they'll fix us anything to eat. I'll bet there are a lot of hungry people on this train." He started up the steps to the dining car.

"You're always hungry," Frank complained. "Even at two in the morning."

Joe halted in surprise just inside the door. "Is it really that late?" he asked, dumbfounded. Even more surprising was the fact that Sally and Ruth were waiting for them. "Hi," he said.

"We were wondering if you'd join us for a hot chocolate," Sally said. "The chef got up and is making a huge vat of it for everyone."

"Come on," Ruth added. "Our treat."

"Last of the big spenders?" Joe said. "Lovely girls, hot chocolate—how about it, Frank?"

"Sounds good to me," Frank said. Besides

Ruth was cute. And she didn't look anything like Talia—or Callie Shaw.

The two girls giggled.

Sally lowered her voice and said, "Do you mind if we ask you a question?"

"What would you like to know?" Joe grinned as he realized that lots of other passengers were staring at them, too.

"Are you guys spies or something?" Sally whispered.

Joe gave his brother a broad wink. "Now that's a long story," he said. "That may take *two* hot chocolates."

Frank and Joe's next case:

A vacation in Laguna Beach, California, together with a big-time volleyball tournament in the sun and sand, have put the Hardys in seventh heaven. The action promises to be hard and fast and fun—so what could possibly go wrong? Nothing . . . until the games begin and murder takes a hand!

The Frosty Soft Drink Company is sponsoring the event to promote their new sports drink, Hi-Kick. But the contest has turned into a tournament of terror, and one competitor has already paid with his life. Frank and Joe will have to high kick *their* game into high gear—before the cost of a cold drink puts someone else on ice . . . in *Spiked!*, Case #58 in The Hardy Boys Casefiles™.

SUPER HIGH TECH ... SUPER HIGH SPEED ... SUPER HIGH STAKES!

VICTOR APPLETON

He's daring, he's resourceful, he's cool under fire. He's Tom Swift, the brilliant teen inventor racing toward the cutting edge of high-tech adventure.

Tom has his own lab, his own robots, his own high-tech playground at Swift Enterprises, a fabulous research lab in California where every new invention is an invitation to excitement and danger.

- ☐ **TOM SWIFT 1 THE BLACK DRAGON** ....67823/$2.95
- ☐ **TOM SWIFT 2 THE NEGATIVE ZONE** ....67824/$2.95
- ☐ **TOM SWIFT 3 CYBORG KICKBOXER** ....67825/$2.95
- ☐ **TOM SWIFT 4 THE DNA DISASTER** ....67826/$2.95
- ☐ **TOM SWIFT 5 MONSTER MACHINE** ....67827/$2.99

Simon & Schuster Mail Order Dept. VAA
200 Old Tappan Rd., Old Tappan, N.J. 07675

Please send me the books I have checked above. I am enclosing $_____ (please add 75¢ to cover postage and handling for each order. Please add appropriate local sales tax.) Send check or money order—no cash or C.O.D.'s please. Allow up to six weeks for delivery. For purchases over $10.00 you may use VISA: card number, expiration date and customer signature must be included.

Name _____

Address _____

City _____ State/Zip _____

VISA Card No. _____ Exp. Date _____

Signature _____ 246-04